There was silence for such a lo  *re*
was a problem with Carl's *se*
asked, "And so what happens *oo*
young to actually have a baby

Defying all laws of inertia, the acceleration of Kennedy's heart rate crashed to a halt like a car plowing into a brick wall. "What do you mean?"

"Like, what if you're too young but you still get pregnant?"

"How young?" Kennedy spoke both words clearly and slowly, as if rushing might drive the timid voice away for good.

"Like thirteen."

Praise for *Unplanned*
by Alana Terry

"Deals with **one of the most difficult situations a pregnancy center could ever face**. The message is **powerful** and the story-telling **compelling**." ~ William Donovan, *Executive Director Anchorage Community Pregnancy Center*

"Alana Terry does an amazing job tackling a very **sensitive subject from the mother's perspective**." ~ Pamela McDonald, *Director Okanogan CareNet Pregnancy Center*

"**Thought-provoking** and intense ... Shows **different sides of the abortion argument**." ~ Sharee Stover, *Wordy Nerdy*

"Alana has a way of sharing the gospel **without being preachy**." ~ Phyllis Sather, *Purposeful Planning*

She wouldn't be victimized again. She had to get away. She wouldn't let him catch up to her. A footstep on the concrete. Not a fabrication. Not this time. It was real. Real as the scientific method. Real as her parents' love for her. Real as death. In the pitch darkness, she rushed ahead, running her fingers along the grimy wall so she would know which way to go as she sprinted down the walkway. What did contracting a few germs compare to getting murdered?

How close was he now? And why couldn't she have remembered her pepper spray? She strained her ears but only heard the slap of her boots on the walkway, the sound of her own panting, the pounding of her heart valves in her pericardial sac. She didn't want to stop, couldn't slow down, but she had to save her strength. She needed energy to fight back when he caught up. She couldn't hear him, but that didn't mean he wasn't coming.

Any second now.

Praise for *Paralyzed*
by Alana Terry

"Alana Terry has **done the almost unthinkable**; she has written a story with **raw emotions of real people**, not the usual glossy Christian image." ~ Jasmine Augustine, Tell Tale Book Reviews

"Alana has a way of **using fiction to open difficult issues** and make you think." ~ Phyllis Sather, Author of *Purposeful Planning*

"Once again, Ms. Terry brings a **sensitive but important issue to the forefront** without giving an answer. She **leaves it up to the reader** to think about and decide." ~ Darla Meyer, Book Reviewer

Dedicated to the selfless police officers who courageously serve and protect. May the Lord bless you and keep you safe.

Note: The views of the characters in this novel do not necessarily reflect the views of the author.

The characters in this book are fictional. Any resemblance to real persons is coincidental. No part of this book may be reproduced in any form (electronic, audio, print, film, etc.) without the author's written consent.

www.alanaterry.com

Policed

a novel by Alana Terry

"The Lord works righteousness
and justice for all the oppressed."
Psalm 103:6

CHAPTER 1

Kennedy rolled down the car window. "How about next time we don't wait until halfway into the semester to go out. Deal?" When Reuben didn't respond, she glanced over at him in the passenger seat. "What are you thinking about?"

His face lit up with his usual bright smile. "Nothing. Just next year."

"Almost sophomores. Can you believe it? And we haven't gone insane yet. Well, at least you haven't." She had to laugh. It was embarrassing enough that she went to meet with a campus psychologist once a week. If she couldn't find at least some humor in her situation, she was in big trouble. In fact, it was Reuben who had encouraged her to take her mental health more seriously, and she was forced to begrudgingly admit something she was doing must be helping. She'd only had two panic attacks all semester. Not too bad considering everything she'd gone through this school year.

But she didn't want to think about any of that. Not tonight. It was only Thursday, not even the weekend yet, but she and

Reuben had just finished their chemistry midterm and were on their way to the Opera House to see the Elton John musical *Aida*. They'd been planning for weeks on this date.

Ok, so maybe not a date. Not a real one. Then again, Reuben had texted her yesterday, said he had something important he wanted to tell her tonight. Said she couldn't let him back out. Couldn't let him change his mind and stay silent. She'd lost several hours of sleep trying to figure out what he was about to divulge.

Maybe that's why he was quiet this evening. Beneath his cheerful personality, Reuben could be almost as serious as Kennedy. Her roommate Willow was always teasing both of them for being so studious. Always asking when Kennedy would start dating Reuben for real, but of course, Kennedy never had a good enough answer.

"He's either stuck in the Victorian era, or he's gay," Willow would quip. Kennedy had gotten used to her roommate's teasing, though. And tonight she wasn't going to spoil the atmosphere with negativity from anyone or anything. Wasn't that what her counselor always said? Only let positive energy in, or some psychobabble like that. She figured if seeing the campus quack helped her sit through a calculus lecture without turning into a wheezing, sobbing mess, it was worth the hassle and the time. Besides, as soon as Kennedy mentioned the words *post-traumatic stress disorder* to her missionary parents, they threatened to fly all the way to Massachusetts from China to help her get connected with the services she needed.

Or the services everyone else thought she needed.

It was funny how she was the one who survived a kidnapping and two separate attempts on her life, and everyone assumed she was a big, blaring psychological mess. What about her roommate? What about Willow, who had slept with every single boy in the theater department by now? Who was going to shrink-analyze this karma-fearing, yoga-practicing, granola-crunching pothead roommate from Alaska and tell her all her deviant behavior was the result of early childhood trauma or rubbish like that?

And what about Reuben? There wasn't much Kennedy wouldn't give to gain unbridled access to his psyche, to figure out what caused those quiet, moody spells that sometimes came over him. He hardly talked about his family or upbringing in Kenya unless it was to boast about the birth of his most recent niece or nephew back home. Of course, there were other things she'd want to know too, but they would have to wait until he was ready to tell her.

Like tonight?

The two of them had been through so much together

since they met at their freshman orientation last fall. Two kids who grew up on different continents, both living oceans away from their families, doing their best to stay afloat in Harvard's rigorous pre-med program.

She didn't know when it happened. Maybe one night when they stayed up late working on calculus at the library. Maybe one day in the student union as they scurried to finish a write-up for chem lab. Maybe during one of Kennedy's panic attacks, when Reuben's calm assurance brought her back to reality, helped her recover from the scars and wounds of last semester.

She didn't know when it happened, but Kennedy knew she'd found true friendship. Closer than she'd ever experienced before. Nobody could make her laugh like Reuben. Nobody else would argue literature with her like he did. After spending their first semester at Harvard studying calculus and chemistry side by side, they decided to both enroll in a children's literature course during their spring semester. Together, they had discussed the stereotypic gender roles of the Alden children as they raised themselves in an abandoned boxcar and analyzed *The Giver* until there wasn't a single phrase in Lois Lowry's weirdly dystopian novel that they hadn't dissected. One day Kennedy realized she'd found more than a best friend.

4

She'd found a soul mate.

She only hoped that whatever secret he was planning to tell her tonight was the same secret she'd kept hidden, even from herself, until recently. A giddy, nervous energy zinged up her leg. She really should pay more attention to the road. After growing up on the mission field in Yanji, China, Kennedy hadn't learned to drive until her pastor taught her over Christmas break. She had just gotten her license and still wasn't used to Cambridge driving, with all its funny rotaries and ridiculously congested streets. That was another reason she and Reuben had chosen to go out on a weeknight. Traffic wouldn't be so bad. Besides, they were borrowing Willow's car, and the chances of Kennedy's roommate staying in on a weekend were about as high as Matilda from the Roald Dahl book getting detention for failing a math test.

"So, did you finish reading *My Side of the Mountain* yet?" Reuben asked.

Kennedy was grateful to hear the usual conversational tone in his voice. "We weren't going to talk about school, remember."

"I thought that only applied to math and science," he replied. "By the way, how's your sociology class going?"

Kennedy didn't know why she'd done it, but she let her roommate talk her into taking one of Professor Hill's courses on the American racial divide to fulfill a humanities requirement. On the one hand, it was nice getting to know Willow and a few of her friends better, but the course itself wasn't at all what she'd been hoping for. After reading the catalog description, she assumed the class would be about Martin Luther King, Jr. and the Million Man March. She quickly found out Professor Hill was far more interested in citing every single instance of perceived discrimination that had occurred across the nation in the past three months than delving into America's segregated history.

Kennedy shrugged. "It's all right. I've gotten A's on most of my papers, but I think that's just because I've learned how to write the way she wants and skew everything from the right angle. Actually, the left angle."

The pun was lost on Reuben, who spoke English as his second language, but Kennedy didn't mind. She'd spent the past ten years in southeast China and didn't understand a decent amount of slang or the majority of pop culture references either, so she could empathize with him. She often felt that she had more in common with Reuben, an exchange student from Kenya, than she did with her American peers. On more than one occasion, she wondered if she would have ever made it through her first year at Harvard if it weren't for his friendship.

"What kind of papers do you write for that class?" he asked as Kennedy merged onto Soldier's Field Road.

"A lot of fluff, really. Every week, we have to take something that happened to us personally and explain the racism implicit in the event. Like once, do you remember when you forgot your meal card at the student union and you didn't have any other ID? I wrote that up about how since you're black, the cashier automatically assumed you weren't trustworthy and wouldn't let you give her your student ~~union~~ number, blah, blah, blah. Three pages of drivel about the racial injustices implicit in our interactions with the gray-haired lunch lady who knits socks for her grandkids on her breaks."

Reuben laughed. "You really said that?"

She shrugged. "It was for the grade."

"Do you believe it?" he asked.

"No. But it's what Hill wants to hear, and it's a pretty easy class, so I won't complain too much. It's kind of a joke though. I mean, they take all these cases where people just run into bad luck or something, and they turn every single one of them into an example of racism."

"Like the meal card?"

Kennedy nodded. "Yeah. I mean, if I forget my card and she says I can't give her my number, I figure she's having a

7

bad day. Or maybe her boss is telling her to stop doing that anymore. Either way, I don't assume it's racism. But if she refuses to let a black student give her the number, all of a sudden she's a bigot."

"So do you think America still has a problem with racism?" he asked.

Kennedy had asked herself that same question several times in Professor Hill's class. "Maybe sometimes, but not like it used to. Take Pastor Carl. He and Sandy got married in the South back when blacks and whites hardly ever even dated. They've shared some of their stories with me. It wasn't pretty. But this is a different era. I mean, you look at Carl and all he does, and he's the last person to point fingers and say some big, burly white man is keeping him down."

Kennedy frowned. Had she offended Reuben? Before taking Hill's class, she wouldn't have even asked herself that question, but now all the guilt she'd absorbed from being told how anyone with her complexion had inherited an incurably racist constitution, she wasn't so sure. "I know it can be harder for black people to have some of the same opportunities, especially when we're talking about kids from inner cities. But my guess is most of that's related to poverty and education and things like that. It's a socioeconomic issue, not a racial one."

Had she expressed herself correctly? Why did she feel so nervous? If anything, Hill's class made her feel more uncomfortable talking about race with a black man. Or what was she supposed to call Reuben? She couldn't say *African-American*, since he wasn't a US citizen. Why did it have to be so complicated? She decided to steer the conversation in a new direction. "What about in Kenya? Is there much racism there? Or reverse racism against whites or anything?"

"Not really. The white people who travel to Kenya are either tourists who come with lots of spending money or missionaries who start up schools or hospitals, so white and black relations are pretty good. There's still a lot of prejudice between different tribes though."

Kennedy kept her mouth shut so she wouldn't say something ignorant. Up until now, she hadn't thought about how Kenya's tribal past would still have implications on its society today. She glanced at the clock on Willow's dashboard and then saw blue and red flashing lights in her rearview mirror. Some cop was trying to pass. She merged over to the right.

"What's he doing?" she mumbled when she saw the police car switch lanes with her. She checked her speedometer. She couldn't have been speeding. Traffic was too congested. "Is he blinking at me?"

A familiar, unsettling quiver started in the base of her abdomen. No, she couldn't give in to anxiety right now. She had made so much progress moving on from the trauma of last semester. She was healthy. Whole. She could see a policeman without giving in to flashbacks of her abduction. She could get pulled over without her mind convincing her she was back in a car chase, fleeing for her life while bullets shattered the windows around her.

Couldn't she?

She slowed Willow's car down to a stop. The police pulled up directly behind her.

Great.

"I wonder what I was doing."

Maybe Willow's registration had expired. It sounded like something her roommate would let happen.

"What's taking so long?" Kennedy glanced in the rearview mirror. The policeman still hadn't gotten out of his car. She turned to Reuben. "I'm really sorry. We might be late. Maybe I should hop out and explain to him we're in a hurry."

Reuben raised his eyebrows. "I think we better stay here."

She sighed. This was supposed to be a fun night out together. Well, at least it would be memorable. She wondered what Willow would say when she heard they'd gotten pulled over in her car. She didn't know anything about traffic laws and write-up procedures. Would the ticket go to her or Willow? Kennedy would find a way to pay it regardless, but she didn't want it to count against Willow's record in any way.

Finally, the policeman sauntered over to them. He had that typical side-to-side gait Kennedy always associated with cops in movies. Mr. Bow Legs. She tried to remember from the police shows she watched with her dad what she was supposed to do now. Keep her hands on the wheel? No, that was only for suspects and criminals. This was just a traffic stop. Kennedy had replayed every move she'd made since she turned onto Arlington. Not a single mistake. It had to be something to do with Willow's car. She held her eyes shut for a moment. That was so like her roommate. Why couldn't Willow learn a little personal responsibility?

Officer Bow Legs rapped on her window. His hands were massive. Another tremor blasted through Kennedy's abdomen. She forced herself to take a breath from deep within her belly. While her psychologist was busy probing Kennedy's past — certain that her missionary-kid upbringing overseas was the real culprit for her PTSD and not the fact that two different men had tried to kill her last semester — Kennedy had found a few websites with practical advice to ward off panic attacks.

Inhale through the nose. Expand your belly.

Her three-hundred-buck-a-session shrink would be shocked to learn it could all come down to a few simple breathing techniques.

Kennedy rolled down the window. Her first inclination was to apologize to the officer, but somewhere in the back of her head, she remembered her dad warning her about assuming culpability. Or was that only if you'd been in an accident?

The policeman was glaring at her. She did her best to keep her face neutral, reminding herself she had nothing to be scared of. She hadn't done anything wrong. It wasn't dark yet, but the cop held up his flashlight and shined it into the cabin of the car. Reuben shielded his eyes.

"Hands behind your head!" Mr. Bow Legs shouted at him.

"He was just keeping the light …"

"You shut up," the policeman snapped.

Kennedy glanced over to Reuben who had interlaced his hands behind his head.

"Where's your driver's license?"

12

Kennedy reached for her purse in the center console.

"Get your hands on the wheel!" Bow Legs barked. How far behind were Willow's car tags?

Kennedy hoped he couldn't see her exasperation. Or was that fear? "I was going to show you my license."

"All I asked was where it was."

She peeked at the time. She and Reuben had to find a parking spot right next to the Opera House and be at will call in fifteen minutes if they wanted to catch the show. It would be best to comply. Cops had hard jobs. She had seen them risk their lives for her on more than one occasion. Bow Legs was probably extra tense after a long day at work. The least she could do is make this stop as easy as possible.

"My driver's license is in my purse." She nodded toward it and noted the cop's whole body tense when she moved.

"Where's the registration?" he demanded.

"I don't know. This is my roommate's car." She didn't bother to tell him she wasn't sure what exactly a registration looked like or how she'd recognize one if she saw it.

"Does she know you're driving it?"

Kennedy thought he was trying to make a joke until she saw his deep-set scowl. She answered with a simple, "Yes."

"But you don't know where her registration is?"

"No," Kennedy answered. "Is that why you pulled us over?"

He jerked his head toward Reuben without answering. "Who's that?"

Kennedy glanced at Reuben to see if he would answer for himself.

He didn't.

"This is my friend from school."

The officer glared. "And what's the name of your *friend*?" He made the word sound filthy. Impure.

Reuben lifted his head. "I am Reuben Murunga. I'm a student from Kenya."

"I didn't ask what boat you got off." The cop jerked his head. "All right. Get out of the car."

Kennedy tried to catch Reuben's eye, but he was staring at his lap as he unbuckled his seatbelt. All of Kennedy's questions, all her protests froze in her throat. Her mind taunted her with memories of a trip she took when she was a little girl visiting her grandmother in upstate New York. Someone had burgled the house across the street, and the police were knocking on doors warning the residents to be extra vigilant locking up. Kennedy's dad had called her downstairs, footie pajamas and all, and forced her to shake the officer's hand. "Police are our friends," he told her.

"They're here to help us."

Her dad's words replayed in her mind. *Here to help us.* Well, if she had done something wrong, she would have to accept whatever citation he wrote up for her. That's all there was to it. Her dad would chide her for being careless, but he'd take care of the ticket and that would be that. She just wished she knew what she'd done. Had she forgotten to signal before switching lanes? Is that what this was about?

Here to help us. So why were her insides reeling as fast as a centrifuge machine?

She reached for the car handle when Bow Legs barked, "Just him. You stay put."

She wished Reuben would look at her. What was he thinking? Was he scared? If he was, he was doing a good job hiding it. He opened his door and got out slowly. Methodically. Bow Legs warned him to keep his hands visible, and Reuben held them up by his shoulders the entire time.

Once Reuben was out of the car, the police officer planted one foot behind him. Kennedy recognized the stance from her self-defense course. What did he think, that Reuben was about to attack him?

"All right," he ordered. "Now lace your fingers behind your head. Keep your back to me and take slow steps around the front of the car."

Kennedy kept her fingers on the door handle. "Listen, he wasn't the one driving. I was. If I did something wrong, just let me know so I don't do it again. I already told you, this is my roommate's car, and ..."

"Shut up." The words weren't even a snarl, more like an afterthought. All of Bow Legs' attention was on Reuben. Kennedy probably could have confessed to planting a bomb in Logan Airport and he wouldn't pay any attention.

When Reuben reached the driver's side headlight, the officer planted his hand on his holster. "Stop right there. Don't move."

"Wait, do you really think ..."

Bow Legs wasn't listening to her. He left his post at Kennedy's window and stepped forward. Kennedy tried to pass Reuben some encouraging thought or positive message by sheer will power as the officer lowered Reuben's hands and cuffed them behind his back.

She jumped out of the car. "What are you doing?" Commuter vehicles whizzed up and down Arlington, never slowing down. Didn't anybody see what was happening? Didn't anybody care?

The officer snapped his head around toward Kennedy. "Miss, you need to get back in that car right now."

"No." For once, she was thankful her dad had forced her

to role play through so many ridiculous and embarrassing situations. Of course, he hadn't thought to include a scenario in which Kennedy and her best friend get pulled over and handcuffed without any explanation, but if her dad had taught her anything, it was how to stand up for herself. "You can't just pull someone out of their car like this. He hasn't done anything wrong." She struggled to keep the invasive tinge of hysteria out of her voice but wasn't sure she pulled it off successfully.

"I told you to get back in." Bow Legs' hand was still on his holster. It was enough to dim Kennedy's newfound courage. She shot a desperate glance at the stream of traffic, the blissfully ignorant drivers who didn't even see her. Those who did notice probably assumed she was a drug dealer or some other sort of criminal. The entire situation might be humorous if it weren't so terrifyingly real.

She inched her way backward. "He hasn't done anything wrong." She hadn't tried to sound so whiny. She was thankful her body hadn't given in to a panic attack. Maybe she really had made some progress since last semester. But if she wasn't careful, she was going to start to cry. She refused to be associated with those girls who got out of tickets by summoning the fake tears. Except her tears wouldn't be fake. Fear and confusion coalesced in her gut, washed down by copious volumes of scorching humiliation. She touched the door handle but didn't open it. "What are you going to do?"

Bow Legs' icy scowl could have frozen mercury. He ignored the question and slammed Reuben down against the hood of the car.

"Stop!" Kennedy couldn't even guess what Reuben was feeling right now. His cheek was pressed against Willow's car, his face blocked from view. The only thing that stopped Kennedy from charging the officer was the way one hand still hovered over his holster as he patted Reuben down with his other.

Maybe Professor Hill's course hadn't been as big of a waste of time as Kennedy initially assumed. How many times had the class watched those videos of police officers who overstepped their bounds? Of course, Kennedy had never been able to shake the nagging suspicion that somewhere off the screen, the victims must have done something to aggravate the situation, but what about Reuben? What could he have possibly done to antagonize Bow Legs or deserve any of this?

With a renewed surge of confidence, Kennedy knew what she had to do. She got into the car just like Bow Legs had ordered and pulled out her phone. She would record the whole encounter. That should get the cop to lay off. She started the camera up and set the phone in the pocket of her blouse, hoping it would get the entire scene without the cop noticing.

When she was sure it was recording, she leaned out the window, reminding herself how the people in those police videos had stood up for their rights. "Hey, don't you need some kind of warrant to search somebody?" She wasn't sure if that was true or not, but she remembered her dad saying something about it while they were watching an action movie together.

"Listen, I've heard about enough from you little —." Here the officer let out a string of epithets that insulted both Kennedy and Reuben as well as their ancestry. If this whole incident were racially motivated, at least Bow Legs had offended them both with equal opportunity.

Kennedy licked her lips. Things like this didn't happen to people like her. She had always been at the top of her class. Even after everything she went through last fall, she finished her first semester at Harvard with straight A's except for a single A minus. Bow Legs had no idea what he was doing. This was all some terrible mistake. She stretched her spine as tall as she could manage. "He hasn't done anything wrong, and you need to let us go. Now." Her voice only shook once. "You have no business bothering us like this. We're students at Harvard."

Bow Legs turned to her for the first time. "Yeah, right." He spat out another string of profanities.

"We're going to a show." Kennedy didn't know why she was telling him that. What would he care?

"You're not going to any show, girlie. As soon as I finish searching your car, you and your baboon buddy are coming with me."

"Search us for what?" she demanded. The cars were slowing down now when they passed, and she saw several commuters straining their necks to get a better look. How in the world could anyone mistake people like her and Reuben for criminals?

Bow Legs took a step toward her. "Any more lip out of you, and you'll end up in cuffs too. Got that?" He eyed her up and down. "And just so we're clear, I have no problem giving you a full body search right here on the side of the road if you don't shut up and let me do my job."

Kennedy shot an imploring look at Reuben through the dashboard. Other than a slight twitch in his jaw, he kept himself bent over the hood of the car and didn't move.

The cop opened the door and yanked her out of her seat. She was too surprised to try to free herself from his hold. She bit her lip. The sooner they got this over with, the sooner he'd take those cuffs off Reuben. Right?

He started rummaging under the seats and in the crannies of Willow's car. Kennedy's stomach sank faster than a lead ball. What if he found something Willow or one of her partying friends left behind? What if they thought it belonged to Kennedy and Reuben? More than anything, she wanted to call her dad. He would know what to do.

"There's nothing in there." She knew her voice sounded scared. It probably made her appear even guiltier.

Bow Legs straightened up and slammed the door shut. Good. He hadn't found anything. Her phone was still in her blouse pocket. How much of this encounter would the camera pick up? He stomped to the other side of the car, giving Reuben a harsh nudge when he passed. Kennedy opened her mouth to protest, but Reuben shot her an imploring look that silenced her complaint.

She thought through the similar events she had heard about in Professor Hill's class. Young men getting pulled over and arrested for no reason other than being black. Kennedy had read the accounts, felt sorry for some of the victims, but in the back of her mind had always wondered if they were reading too much into it. Sometimes police pulled people over. They had their reasons. Just because the victim

was black didn't mean it was racially motivated. But this …
What had either of them done?

Bow Legs jerked open the passenger door so hard the
entire car shook. Seconds later, he let out a self-satisfied
grunt and pulled out a Ziploc bag from the glove
compartment. "Not hiding anything, huh?" He was glaring
over the top of the car at Kennedy.

"That's my roommate's. It's her loose-leaf tea."

"Nice try." Bow Legs pocketed the baggie and pulled out
another pair of cuffs. "Come on. You better hope your
eggplant friend has more brains than he looks. You're both
in a world of hurt right about now."

A dozen fears and protests charged through Kennedy's
mind. Were they under arrest? Did they need a lawyer? What
would happen to Reuben? Did he even have the same rights
as an American citizen, or were laws different for
international students? She had gone through enough in the
past year to recognize the surge of adrenaline flooding her
nervous system, but she wasn't sure if it was time for a fight
or flight. Or should she let the cop take them in and trust the
justice system to sort everything out in the end? She was
innocent. Both of them were innocent. So why did it feel like
going with the policeman was tantamount to admitting guilt?
She was even more scared than she'd been when the Chinese

police stopped by her parents' house to question her father about his printing business, his legal front for staying in Yanji as a missionary.

The officer swaggered over to Kennedy. "Come on, Barbie doll. Time to take a little ride."

There's nothing to be scared of, she reminded herself, but she knew it was a lie. There was plenty to be scared of.

"You better start thinking how you're gonna explain that weed."

"It's tea," she insisted again. Kennedy watched Willow prepare it every single morning and had never questioned what was in it. Willow took more supplements than a hypochondriac chiropractor. There was no way Kennedy could keep track of which ingredients were in what concoction. She eyed the bag. Maybe there really was some illegal substance in there. Then what would happen to her? What would happen to Reuben?

Police are our friends. Kennedy could hear her father's voice mentally coaxing her. She wondered if this was the adult equivalent to finding out Santa Claus was a lie your parents perpetuated in a spirit of fun and holiday cheer.

Bow Legs stepped behind Kennedy and waved the bag in her face. "What do you say? Is this worth a night behind bars?" He leaned into her, pressing her body against the car.

She clenched her jaw shut to keep from screaming. Tears of humiliation and hatred stung the corners of her eyes. She held her breath, trying to make her body as small as possible, but the farther she pressed into the car, the more heavily he dug into her.

"Looks like I've got a right to pat you down, don't I?" His breath was hot. Acrid. Kennedy could almost taste it. She fought her gag reflex.

Police are our friends. It was still her father's voice she heard, but now it was taunting. Mocking.

His hands started at her shoulders and lingered as they slid down to her hips. He felt in each of her pants pockets, his pace painstakingly methodical. His hands traveled back up her body slowly, his fingers probing each rib as he worked his way toward her chest. "Nice girl like you wouldn't be hiding anything in here, would you?" he hissed in her ear.

She froze. What did he think he was doing? And how much angrier would he grow when he saw the phone in her pocket? Kennedy recalled a similar simulation from her self-defense course. She could head butt him if she wanted or bring up her heel for a swift kick to his groin. She clenched her eyes shut, unsure which reflex his touch would trigger. But before his groping hands could complete their circuit,

Reuben barged between them.

"Leave her alone."

Without warning, the officer punched Reuben in the gut. Reuben doubled over as Bow Legs brought his knee up to his face. Reuben staggered.

"You dirty n—." Without warning, the cop whipped out his pistol and smashed its butt against Reuben's head. He crumpled to the ground, where the officer's boots were ready to meet him with several well-placed kicks.

Throwing all rational thoughts aside, Kennedy jumped on his back. Anything to get him to stop beating Reuben. The officer swore and swatted at her. Kennedy heard herself screaming but had no idea what she was saying. Her brain zoned in on Bow Legs, the object of all her hatred and disdain. She couldn't see anything else, nor could she understand how it was that when her normal vision returned, she was lying on her back staring at a vaguely familiar face, but the officer and Reuben were nowhere to be seen.

CHAPTER 2

"Just hold steady."

She recognized the man. She knew if it weren't for her splitting headache, she would be able to place him.

"We've met before. It's Ian McAlister." The Good Samaritan held out a bottle of water. "Are you thirsty? I don't want to move your head right now, not until the ambulance gets here, but I could try to get you a small sip."

Ian? Pulses of pain shot through Kennedy's gray matter as she tried to connect his face to the name. She squinted up at his head of red hair, which she recognized from their few encounters last semester. "You're a journalist, right?"

He nodded. "Yeah. You feel ok? Any dizziness? How's your head?"

"It hurts."

"I'm not surprised. Try not to move too much before the paramedics get here. I'm sure they'll want to check you out."

"Where's Reuben?" She struggled to sit up, but Ian and a wave of dizziness both prevented her.

"Someone's with him right now."

Kennedy wished she could see what was happening.

"Don't touch me." It was Reuben's voice. She'd never heard him sound so angry. They weren't arresting him, were they?

"What's going on?" she asked.

Ian frowned. "He's pretty agitated. There's some nurse who pulled over, but he won't let her near him."

"Leave me alone!" Reuben yelled.

Kennedy had to get to him. Had to see what the problem was.

"Sir, I'm trying to help. The back of your head is bleeding. I just want to …"

"Stay back. All of you." Reuben's voice was tense, almost as if he were trying not to cry.

"Is he ok?" Kennedy asked.

"I don't know." Ian glanced at his watch. "The ambulance will be here soon. You'll both get all the attention you need."

"There was a cop," she tried to explain. "He was …"

Ian frowned.

"Did you see anything?" she asked.

"Just you and your friend lying on the asphalt."

It didn't make sense. Where had Bow Legs gone? She

shut her eyes and did what she could to assess her injuries. She could breathe normally. None of her limbs hurt. Aside from the headache and a general achy feel all over, nothing deviated too far from baseline. She took a deep breath and worked through the dizziness until she could sit up. Ian held out his hands as if he wanted to catch her if she fell. "Are you sure you want to be doing that?" he asked.

Kennedy was too focused on keeping her balance to answer. She gritted her teeth and reminded herself she had been through worse pain than this.

Much worse.

She didn't shrug off the journalist, who wrapped his arm around her while she attempted to stand. She let him support her as she worked out her tight muscles and made her way over to Reuben. He was lying on the rocky pavement, no longer cuffed, his head resting in a small puddle of blood. Kennedy untangled herself from Ian's hold.

"Get away from me," Reuben snapped when he saw her.

Kennedy nearly lost her balance. "I just want to …"

He clenched his teeth. "Get back."

She didn't argue, and she didn't resist when Ian tucked an arm around her waist and led her to his car. "You can rest here until the paramedics come."

Kennedy winced as he eased her down into the driver's

seat. "What's wrong with him?" She hadn't been asking about Reuben's injuries so much as his attitude.

Before Ian could answer, a whining ambulance sped toward them and parked. The onlookers dispersed, and three paramedics jumped out the back. Ian pointed at Reuben. "Check him out first."

Kennedy let out her breath and allowed her body to relax a little. Reuben would get the medical attention he needed. Everything would be fine now.

Or would it?

She recalled the cop's roaming hands on her body. She had never felt so violated. Her ears rang with the echoes of his curses and slurs. If she didn't have the entire encounter recorded, she wouldn't believe half of it.

The recording. She reached for her phone in her blouse pocket. The screen blinked with a message. *Memory full. Video failed to record.*

"Everything ok?" Ian asked.

No, it wasn't. After everything they had endured, all the indignity, all the shame, now there wasn't any proof. Memory full? She wasn't sure if she wanted to cry or throw her phone in front of the oncoming traffic.

But maybe it wasn't that bad. Arlington was as crowded as the courtyards of Willie Wonka's chocolate factory the day he reopened his doors. Somebody would have seen. Several somebodies. They could corroborate Kennedy's story.

The cop was long gone. He must had driven off like a coward, leaving Kennedy and Reuben to heal from their injuries. She didn't know his name, but with enough witnesses and police logs, they'd find him.

Right?

She stared at the phone in her lap. Betrayed by a stupid piece of technology. It wasn't fair. None of this was fair. She should have never been pulled over in the first place. And now Reuben ...

"You sure he's going to be all right?" she asked.

Ian's eyes were soft. Like Charlotte's after Wilbur the pig discovered why the farmer was fattening him up. "I'm sure the paramedics will fill you in soon, but I wouldn't worry if I were you."

Kennedy glanced over. The ambulance crew was lifting Reuben onto a gurney.

"I should see if he's ok."

Ian extended his hand. "Want help?"

"No." She winced as she stood up and decided she'd take some Tylenol if the paramedics had any to offer, but otherwise she'd rather have them focus on helping Reuben. She kept her eyes off the puddle of his blood on the cement.

She walked to the side of Reuben's stretcher and took his hand. "Are you ok?"

He pulled away. What was wrong? Did he think this whole thing was her fault? Did he blame her for taking him out in her roommate's car? She had done what she could to stand up for him. His silent treatment bored holes into her chest the size of test tube stoppers.

She stepped aside to let a member of the ambulance crew by. "Is everything all right?" she asked.

The paramedic didn't pause to look at her. "He'll be fine. We're taking him in to Providence now." He hoisted himself into the ambulance.

"Are you the girl who was with him?" his co-worker asked. "You really should let us check you out before you start walking around."

"I'm fine," Kennedy insisted. "I just want to make sure he's ok."

"We're taking him in right now. You're welcome to follow and meet us at Providence if you'd like."

Reuben shook his head. "Just go home. Don't worry about me."

Did he know what he was saying? Was this the kind of brain injury that could alter personalities? Why was he acting this way?

"I'd like to stick around." She wanted to find a discreet way to tell him her dad would probably pay for his medical bills if he was worried about money. All Kennedy had to do was ask.

Reuben jerked his shoulder away when she touched him. "Go home. I'll text you when I get back to campus."

A lump the size of the BFG's big toe had settled at the top of her larynx. "You sure? I don't mind ..."

He scowled. "Just leave me alone."

One of the paramedics shot Kennedy a sympathetic glance. Kennedy stepped aside so they could lift the stretcher into the back of the ambulance. She crossed her arms and watched, expecting any moment for Reuben to change his mind and call her to him. Apologize for his behavior. All she heard was the chatter of the crew as they prepared him for transport.

She was still standing in the same spot when they pulled away. They didn't put on their sirens, which was a good sign. Reuben's injuries couldn't be that serious. So why had he acted so strangely?

It was cold. The wind always seemed fiercest around this part of town anyway.

"Hey, you need a lift or anything?"

Surprised by the voice, Kennedy turned to face Ian.

She had forgotten the journalist was there. He was the only one left. Everyone else had gone. All those potential witnesses ...

"Can I drive you someplace?"

She cringed when he touched her shoulder. She shook her head. All she wanted now was to be alone.

"No, thanks." She tried to force a smile to compensate for the shortness in her voice.

"You sure?"

She gave him one more quick glance and nodded. "Yeah. I'm sure."

He followed her to Willow's car and leaned down once she was in the driver's seat. "Is there anything else I can do for you?"

Kennedy buckled her seatbelt and stared at the empty pavement.

Ian sighed. "I've had experience with this sort of thing. It can get complicated. So just let me know if you need me."

Kennedy turned the key in the ignition. "As a member of the press?"

He shrugged. "Or as a listening ear. It's up to you." He passed her a business card. Until then, she hadn't realized anyone younger than her dad still carried those things around.

"Thanks." Kennedy hoped he didn't take her brusque departure too personally. She shut the door and managed to drive about a mile and a half before she pulled over into a gas station, where she tried to wash away her fears and frustrations with a series of choking, heaving sobs.

CHAPTER 3

"No, he never told us his name." Kennedy was still parked in front of the gas station where she had finally decided to call her parents in Yanji.

"Well, I'm sorry," she replied to her dad's reprimand. "It's not like I wake up every day and tell myself to ask for the name of every single cop who pulls me over and starts kicking my friend on the side of the road."

She could hear her mom sigh on the other end of the line. "You know you're going to have to report this, don't you?"

Kennedy's stomach was twisting and twirling like a double helix. "How can I do that if I don't even know the guy's name?"

"They have records of their traffic stops, sweetie. All you have to do is tell the police department where you were and what time it was when you got pulled over."

Kennedy didn't try to keep the sarcastic barbs out of her tone. "And then he can say it wasn't him and make me and Reuben out to be liars." In spite of all her arguments, she knew her mom was right. She'd have to file a report, but she didn't even know how to begin. Was she just supposed to waltz into the station and ask to speak to the cop in charge of complaints?

"But his superiors will have the record of him pulling you over," Kennedy's mom insisted, "and you'll have the paramedic workers there to verify that's where your friend was injured. That's evidence enough in anybody's book."

Her father cleared his throat. "Not if the officer failed to call in before he stopped. That would explain why there wasn't any backup. Cops do it all the time, pull someone over and unless they write a ticket, there's no paper trail, no proof whatsoever."

"But she can't just go on as if none of this ever happened …" Her parents went back and forth, but their voices were too low for Kennedy to hear most of their bickering.

"All right," her dad finally said, "here's what we're going to do. I'm going to call my friend's son Taylor. He's a state trooper out somewhere in Alaska, but before that he was on the police force in Waltham. I'll get in touch with Taylor, run everything by him, ask what he thinks you should do. Sometimes these cops, they got this unwritten code. Work together to keep each other out of trouble, make a big mess for anyone who challenges the status quo."

So much for his *policemen are our friends* mantra.

"But what about Reuben?" Kennedy noticed the whine in her voice but couldn't control it. "He hurt him really bad. By the time I realized what was going on, the cop was already gone, and Reuben was on the ground, and ..."

"You said he's at the hospital, right?" her dad asked. "I'm sure they'll have the police meet him there so he can give his story. And the paramedics said he was going to be fine. You'll just have to take their word for it."

But he didn't even want to talk to me. Kennedy kept the thought to herself. Some things were too painful to speak out loud. Why did her parents have to live so far away?

"Listen," Kennedy's mom inserted, "are you busy tonight? Do you have any homework you need to get done by tomorrow?"

"No. Reuben and I were going to see *Aida*. We got the tickets two months ago ..." She cut herself off before her voice betrayed her.

"Ok then," said her mom. "Here's what I want you to do. I want you to drive yourself over to Carl and Sandy's. I was emailing Sandy just a second ago while you were talking with your father. She's already expecting you. I want you to go to Sandy's, take a nice hot shower, do something to relax. Then tomorrow, after your father talks with this trooper guy and gets his opinion, we'll call you back and make some decisions. For now, you just get the rest you need and try not to worry."

Oh yeah. Not worry. That was so like her mom. *Here dear, eat a cookie and all your troubles will vanish.*

"You ok, Kensie girl?" her dad asked.

Kennedy shut her eyes and let out her breath. "Yeah," she lied.

"Oh," her mom piped, "I just heard back from Sandy. She wants to know do you want her to come pick you up?"

"I don't know. I need to get Willow her car back."

"Are you well enough to drive safely?" her dad asked.

"Yeah."

"Then go over to Carl and Sandy's now and take the car back with you to campus later on. Ok?"

When she lived at home, she hated the way her dad had so many rules, so many protocols for everything, but now it was nice to have a simple plan to follow. Why had she spent so much energy in high school complaining about her family?

She spent a few extra minutes convincing her mother she was really ok before telling her parents good night and hanging up. She thought about sending Reuben a text but decided against it.

Get herself to Carl and Sandy's. If there was anyone in the Boston-Cambridge area who knew how to pamper her, it was her pastor's family. A night sipping tea with Sandy or listening to Carl's booming preacher's voice impart some wisdom or inspiration was just what she needed.

She took a deep breath and reminded herself that after everything she'd been through tonight, she should be proud she hadn't had a single panic attack. She sped up before merging onto the freeway on her way to the Lindgrens'.

CHAPTER 4

Every time Kennedy glanced at the car's clock, she regretted she wasn't at *Aida* with Reuben. Would they be into the second act by now? She didn't know a whole lot about the Elton John show. She just knew she liked the music samples she'd heard online and it boasted rave reviews and several Tony awards.

Tonight was supposed to be something special, something she and Reuben could look back on and remember for years to come.

What had happened?

She'd dissected every second, from the moment they got into Willow's car until the ambulance drove him away. What had gone wrong?

He had wanted to tell her something, and in her childishness, she'd dared to hope it had to do with their relationship. Had to do with his feelings for her. Part of her would be happy keeping things as they were. She and Reuben worked so well together, and if they started to actually date, there was always the chance of ruining a perfect friendship. But then again, what if they could go even deeper, enjoy each other's company even more fully? It was worth the risk, wasn't it? She thought about the line in *The Last Battle* by C. S. Lewis. "Further up and further in." The representation of exponential improvement. An eternity of ever-increasing joys that carried you closer and closer to infinity, just like an asymptote.

All of her musings were pointless, however. Whatever it was, something had turned Reuben against her. He had done so much for her last semester, helped her through so many trying ordeals. Why would he shut her out now?

She wasn't paying attention to where she was driving and realized she had missed her turn. If she kept going this way, she'd end up at Providence Hospital.

Providence Hospital.

She weighed her options. She could drown her sorrow and confusion over tea and Sandy's homemade desserts, or she could actually talk to Reuben.

She stayed on the freeway.

When she pulled up at the hospital, her muscles were as tight and wound up as a spring scale. She texted the Lindgrens to cancel their plans and practiced a few of her deep breaths before getting out of the car. She could do this.

If she could handle twenty-two Harvard credits and maintain a 3.9 GPA, she could walk into a hospital and offer her friend the emotional support he needed.

The wind had picked up. She clutched her light coat against her chest as her hair whipped across her face. Sometime during her scuffle with the cop, she had lost her barrette. She sighed and tried to envision herself exhaling all her disappointment and anger like those breathing gurus suggested.

It didn't work.

As soon as she stepped inside Providence, she realized she had no idea how to find Reuben. She walked up to the information desk. "Hi, I'm looking for my friend. He came here by ambulance about half an hour ago."

The man behind the booth didn't smile. "Name?"

"Reuben Murunga." She spelled it for him as he typed on his keyboard.

"Looks like they have him in the ER. Do you know the way?"

She didn't answer. Her steps grew slower the closer she got to the emergency room. What was she doing here? Weren't there all kinds of patient privacy laws that would keep her from seeing Reuben, or was that just in movies and TV shows?

When she reached the ER, she wasn't sure who she should talk to, so she rooted herself in line behind a harried mother bouncing a crying baby and a middle-aged man with his arm in a sling. When it was Kennedy's turn, she walked up to the glass partition and explained into the microphone why she had come.

"Let me ask if he's accepting visitors. What's your name?"

"Kennedy Stern."

The triage nurse picked up the phone, but Kennedy couldn't hear the conversation through the partition. The woman hung up and pointed to some empty chairs. "Have a seat. Someone will be out to talk with you shortly."

Kennedy stared for just a moment in hopes of reading the woman's expression. Why would they send someone to talk to her? It seemed like they would either let Kennedy see Reuben or not. Why all the extra meetings and waiting? Did she have to prove she knew him or something?

She sat in a chair and glanced at a young man whose arm was draped around his wife or girlfriend. Kennedy couldn't see her face but could read the sorrow in her posture. The man kept his whole body hunched over as if he wanted to shield her from the world. Fear and grief were written on his face as clearly as the colored pigments on chromatography paper. After a perfectly still moment, he took his finger and lifted some stray hair off the woman's forehead.

Kennedy pried her eyes away from the private scene and glanced at the other faces, the others here waiting. Sometimes it was hard to tell who was here for medical treatment and who had come to offer support. She was one of the only people there by herself.

"Miss Stern." The title sounded foreign. Kennedy glanced up, half expecting to see a nurse ready to escort someone much older into the back rooms. But the man looking directly at her wasn't a nurse.

She stared at the uniformed police officer and wasn't sure if she should stand and go with him or try to run away. Was this what her dad warned her about? Was the cop going to accuse her of drug possession and drag her off to jail?

She glanced around. Several eyes were on her. What did these people think she'd done? There wasn't anywhere she could go.

"You Kennedy Stern?" he asked, and she wondered why he didn't keep his voice down. What happened to confidentiality laws?

She nodded.

He held a door open. "Will you please come with me?"

The hallway branched off in one direction and then

another. Kennedy was lost within her first few turns following him. Each corridor looked the same, each hall so brightly lit she had to squint to keep the light from bouncing off all the bleached white walls and blinding her. Why was she here? What was the cop doing? She'd had enough of policemen for the night.

Maybe for an entire lifetime.

He was silent as he led her down the serpentine corridor, past rows of patient rooms, past vending machines stuffed with high fructose corn syrup, caffeine, and a whole arsenal of artificial ingredients. Her headache had returned with increased fury. Where was Reuben?

The cop opened an unmarked door and held it open. "Right in here, please."

She glanced at his face as she entered the room. Late twenties, maybe, or early thirties. A short, well-kept beard covered his chin, with tinges of copper highlighting the dirty blond. Grayish eyes that were watching her every move. She wanted to hide.

"Have a seat." He gestured to a small couch and then sat in a folding chair across from it. "My name's Dominic."

Strange. She would have expected him to call himself Officer So-and-So. Why the informality? Why the plush seat, the lounge room with a fruit basket and bottled water on an ornate coffee table? Why wasn't he bringing her right to Reuben unless …

Her whole body stiffened as if someone had frozen each of her muscle fibers with liquid nitrogen. This explained everything. Why the triage nurse wouldn't tell her directly how to get to Reuben. Why the officer was using his first name. She glanced around the room, half expecting to see advertisements for funeral homes and pamphlets lying around on how to deal with the loss of a loved one.

She had to know. Had to ask, but her whole body was numb. Is this how Reuben would have felt right before …

"I just got back from seeing your friend."

Kennedy held on to his words like a drowning lab rat would clutch at a floating island.

"In case you were worried," Dominic continued, "he's doing fine. Getting a few stitches, and then it's home." He glanced at his notebook. "Well, back to his dorm, I guess. He's from …" His eyes scanned the page.

"Nairobi," Kennedy answered.

"Nairobi?" Dominic glanced at his pad of paper, but even when he wasn't looking right at her, Kennedy got the feeling he could read her mind. He stared at her with the same intensity her therapist showed when she first mentioned she was the daughter of Christian missionaries. "Right. So." He clasped his hands to his knees and leaned forward. "Do you want to tell me what happened tonight?"

Reuben was fine, but confusion clouded Kennedy's relief. Why was the cop asking her? Did he doubt Reuben's story? Warning signals zinged through Kennedy's cerebrum. Hadn't her dad warned her about cops who make it hard for people who rat out other cops? Is that what this was? Is that why she couldn't visit Reuben, why he brought her all the way down here to some secluded room …

"I'd really like to check on my friend first, if that's all right with you." Why did she add that last part? Shouldn't she be more assertive? What made this officer think he had the right to isolate her, intimidate her …

"You're welcome to check with the nurse when we're finished," he said, "but last I heard, he was refusing visitors."

That probably only referred to cops like you. Kennedy knew better than to speak the thought out loud. She ran through the entire encounter on Arlington. She didn't remember the details of the fight itself, but she recalled something about jumping on the officer's back. If she was going to get in trouble for that, why hadn't Bow Legs arrested her himself? Why did he just run away? Probably because he was a coward who knew he was in the wrong.

He's the one who punched Reuben. The one who kicked him when he was down. Kennedy was only trying to help, and Reuben wouldn't have given the officer any trouble if he hadn't tried to grope Kennedy like that. Reuben was defending her. She was defending him. She was sure the public would see it that way, but of course her phone had betrayed her with its stupid memory. Why hadn't she taken the time to erase some of those dumb photos of lab results or lecture notes leftover from last semester?

Kennedy hadn't done anything wrong. The more she replayed the entire encounter, the more firmly she believed in her innocence. But would other policemen see it that way? Somewhere in the back of her mind, she remembered a campy cop movie she'd watched with her dad back in Yanji. A jaded long-time officer was explaining departmental policy to his new rookie partner. "You take a swing at one of us, there's no way you're walking into the police station on your own two feet. Not by the time we get done with you." At the time, she'd just thought the threat was for dramatic effect, but after her dad's warning, she wondered if that same unwritten code persisted even in a city as supposedly progressive as Boston.

She studied Dominic's face, trying to read him. If this was some kind of a good cop/bad cop routine like in TV shows or detective novels, he seemed better suited for the part of the good guy. The friendly one. The one who'll make sure you're comfortable and offer you bottled water and keep his expression open and engaged, like he'd taken hours of departmental training in active listening.

What would happen if she didn't comply? Would he turn into a raging maniac, threaten her with every single punishment he could legally throw at her? Or maybe there was a partner hiding in another room ready to take over if this nice-guy performance failed.

Kennedy fidgeted with her phone in her pocket, wondering what she should do. Could she ask him for a chance to call her dad first, or would that just make her look guilty?

Dominic leaned forward. "So, you ready to talk about it?"

No, she wasn't ready. In fact, there was a decent chance she would never be ready. Not like this. For the briefest second, she wondered if he was even supposed to be asking her questions without a lawyer present.

Please God, she begged, *show me a way out of this.*

Her phone vibrated in her hand and then let out a little beep. She glanced at the screen. It was a text from Reuben. *If the police ask you any questions, I haven't told them anything.*

She slipped her cell back in her pocket.

"Who was that?" the officer asked.

"Just my roommate." Kennedy tried to meet his eyes. Wouldn't most cops be able to tell when someone was lying? "It was her car I was in tonight, and she was just ..."

"Yeah, the car," Dominic interrupted. "Maybe we can start there."

Kennedy stared at her lap as if the answers to all his questions might magically appear on her jeans. Why was this so difficult? Her dad had told her to wait before complaining to the police. He didn't tell her what to do if they stopped and questioned her. Why had she thought it'd be a good idea to come here at all? She could be on her third cup of tea at the Lindgrens' by now.

Dominic let out a loud sigh. "How about this. Let's start with me telling you what I know, and then you can tell me what you know."

Yeah, he was definitely taking the good-cop angle.

He leaned back in his chair. "All I know is I've got a patient back there with injuries consistent with what you'd see in an assault. He gets in the ambulance, refuses to answer any questions, won't tell anyone why or how he got hurt. Let's call that exhibit A." He gestured with his hands. "Then over here, we've got exhibit B. Exhibit B is two calls we got from drivers very concerned when they saw a white police officer kicking a black male on the side of the road." He leveled his eyes. "What's really interesting is the drivers were calling from Arlington, and one of the very next calls our operator got was for an ambulance to pick up an injured black male from that very same stretch of road."

He crossed its arms. "So that's what I know. Would you care to take a turn?"

Kennedy was too busy praying for some sort of deliverance to put her thoughts into any coherent order. She stared at the floor and wondered what kind of baked goodies Sandy would have made tonight. She fidgeted with her hands in her lap. "We got pulled over." She couldn't bring her eyes to his. "The officer made Reuben get out of the car. Put him in cuffs." She willed her body to keep as calm as possible. If the story had to come out, it would do so without the interruptions of tears and dramatics.

Dominic still leaned forward. Did he believe her?

"And then I tried to stop him, said we hadn't done anything wrong, so he made me get out of the car too, and …" Her throat clenched shut, her mind reeling with the sensation of the officer's hands sliding up and down her hips and sides. The putrid stink of his stale breath. The heat from his whispered words, venomous like a hissing snake.

The trembling that had settled into her core all the way back at Arlington now found its way to her limbs. There was no way to hide this kind of reaction from the cop. He'd believe her or he wouldn't. Either way, he'd know how upset she was by the entire ordeal.

She couldn't bring herself to talk about Bow Legs' groping hands slithering up and down her body. She shook her head as if that might convince her brain the entire thing was fictional, the results of an overactive imagination coupled with the exaggerated stories she'd studied in Professor Hill's class. Tears spilled down her cheeks. It was a good thing she hated the caking feel of mascara and never wore the stuff.

If Dominic was surprised or annoyed by her behavior, he didn't show it. "So he made you both get out of the car, put your friend in cuffs, and then?"

Kennedy wanted to go home. Go back to her dorm, take a hot shower, and change her clothes. Forget how degraded she'd felt. Forget how scared she'd been for Reuben's safety.

"Reuben was trying to help me." She was close to sobbing now, but she'd stopped caring. Someone was here, listening to her story, someone who had the power to free Reuben from any charges and punish the real culprit. "He hadn't done anything wrong. He was just trying to help me."

Dominic's open expression turned downward into the slightest trace of a frown. "Protect you from what?"

In a flash, the memory became suffocating. Bow Legs, with all his offensive slurs and leering looks, loomed larger in her mind than he could have possibly been in real life. She couldn't shake him off. A loud gasp. A desperate attempt to suck in air after her lungs had already decided to clench themselves shut. If she couldn't breathe, she couldn't feel. If she couldn't feel, she'd forget the humiliation. The filthy, slimy shame that seeped through her clothes by osmosis, poisoning her bloodstream.

Dominic had crouched beside her and was holding an open bottle to her lips. Twelve ounces of glacial water would never be enough to wash away the hot searing trauma of tonight's events. The entire Bering Glacier wouldn't be enough.

She took a delicate sip, forcing her lungs to calm down enough that she could swallow the tepid liquid. There was a small fraction of her brain — five, or maybe ten percent if she felt like being generous — that was replaying all the information from those self-help websites, all that mumbo jumbo about cleansing breaths and diaphragm engagement. The rest of her mental energy was focused on projecting an increasingly odious image of Bow Legs throughout her entire consciousness, an image that only grew larger as it fed on her fear.

Dominic was rubbing her back. "Hey, you're safe now. Nobody here wants to hurt you." She was glad he didn't offer the usual barrage of senseless advice: *Don't worry. Just calm down. You're ok.*

She wasn't ok. She was glad he didn't feel the need to convince her otherwise.

Her back and shoulders heaved as her lungs wheezed air in and out. Tears splashed on Kennedy's lap and on Dominic's hand that still held out the bottle of water. She wanted to apologize to him, but what would be the point?

"Are you a person of faith?" It was a strange question to ask in the middle of a conference room behind the ER.

She nodded. "I'm a Christian." She was almost ashamed to admit it. What kind of testimony was she offering while blubbering like this?

Dominic slid beside her on the couch. "Me too. I don't want to make you uncomfortable, but I was wondering if I could pray for you. I can tell you're shaken up."

In different circumstances, she might have laughed at his polite euphemism.

"Would that be ok with you?"

She didn't have much faith that a simple prayer from a

stranger would do anything to ease tonight's trauma or cure her anxiety, but at least it would give her a break from this interrogation. It could give her the chance she needed to collect herself before the interview proceeded any further. She nodded her consent and bowed her head.

Dominic didn't jump right into a prayer like she expected. He sat beside her quietly for what felt like several minutes. She wondered if she'd misunderstood him. Maybe he just wanted to pray for her silently. Oh, well. As long as it meant she got a break from answering his questions or feeling like a fool while she blubbered away on the couch, she'd take it.

Apparently, however, he wasn't planning on remaining silent the whole time. He didn't begin with any formal opening, no flowery greeting to make sure everyone in earshot knew who he was talking to. But the words that flowed out of his mouth were almost like Scripture itself.

Powerful. Majestic. Inspiring.

She recognized a few Bible verses woven into his words, but it didn't feel forced or artificial. And the way he prayed made Kennedy wonder if he knew all about her. Had he read about her in the news after the kidnapping last fall? Maybe he went to Carl's church and she just hadn't ever seen him there.

Kennedy had lived her whole life hearing Christians pray

for healing. *Lord, help Tyson's hurt tummy. Give the doctors wisdom when Aunt Lilian goes in for her biopsy. God, please help Grandma not die from cancer.* But she'd never experienced a prayer like this. It was as if Dominic were a surgeon, searching out the sickness, zoning in on each individual injured spots. He began broadly, praying for Kennedy's peace of mind, for comfort from whatever had made her feel afraid.

And then it grew more specific. Prayers for her mind. Prayers for wholeness. For healing. Dominic interrupted his petition to ask Kennedy if he could put his hand on her forehead. She surprised herself by agreeing. Something in her was hungry for the faith, the power she experienced in Dominic's prayer. Her body tingled with an inexplicable electric power, and when he rested his palm against her skin, the whole area radiated heat and energy.

He asked God for soundness of mind. Asked God for freedom. At the mention of freedom, a quiver coursed through her being. Dominic must have felt it too. He prayed even more fervently for release. Deliverance. Hope surged up in Kennedy's chest. Swelling. Like the giant ocean breakers crashing into the Hispaniola when Jim Hawkins set sail with Captain Smollett, Long John Silver, and his crew of mutineers in *Treasure Island.*

Dominic spoke against fear. Spoke against anxiety. He prayed against the trauma of Kennedy's past, and for the first time she understood what Christians mean when they call somebody a prayer warrior. Up until that moment, Kennedy assumed it was an honorary title given to people who really liked to talk to God. Tonight, she realized that prayer wasn't just a discipline. It wasn't something like flossing your teeth that you're supposed to do because it's good for you.

Tonight, she understood that prayer was a battle. At first, she had compared Dominic to a doctor. Now, she realized he was also a soldier. And not just an enlisted man who could follow orders and carry a gun. He was a warrior, a warrior who for some reason or other had decided to go to battle for her in a way nobody else in Kennedy's entire life ever had. Growing up in the church, Kennedy had sat under a dozen Sunday school teachers or more. Why hadn't any of them taught her to pray like this? Nobody she'd ever known prayed like this, not even her own parents, faithful missionaries by anyone's definition of the term. Maybe if Kennedy had spent more time in her family's prayer meetings instead of shopping the Yanji clothes stores with her friends she would have heard intercession like this, but she doubted it.

Dominic took his hand off Kennedy's forehead, and she realized the prayer was over. Her skin no longer burned where he had touched her, but a halo of warmth and peace settled around her. She didn't know what she was supposed to say but realized she was breathing evenly again. She couldn't recall when or how the panic attack ended. She stared at Dominic, half expecting him to disappear from sight or transfigure into an angelic being while she sat watching. He looked so ordinary and unassuming.

Who was this man?

He was a cop. He belonged to the same department as the one who had accosted her and Reuben. But she'd never met anyone like him before. She'd never heard anyone pray for her like that. Not even Pastor Carl, the godliest man she knew in the States.

What did Dominic have that every other Christian lacked?

"You feeling a little better now?"

It was strange to hear Dominic asking her a question. His voice, which just minutes ago had transformed itself into a weapon of spiritual warfare, was so normal now. He looked even more average than he had when they first met, a slightly tired expression clinging around his hazel eyes.

Kennedy nodded. "Thanks for praying for me. It helped."

It was a lame thing to say, but how else was she supposed to respond? She still wasn't quite sure what had happened to her. Had she just imagined that heat on her forehead when his hand touched her?

Dominic smiled. Such a straightforward, unassuming smile. Did he know what he'd just done for her? Did he know what sort of power his soul possessed? "Now, about your story ..."

So this was it. This was the part when the good-cop skit ended and he demanded to know why she jumped on the back of a uniformed policeman who was just out doing his job. She inhaled. At least her spirit still maintained a shred of the peace that had wrapped itself around her during his prayer.

She was ready. As ready as she'd ever be.

Dominic scratched at his beard. "So, you said earlier this policeman attacked you after pulling you over and cuffing your friend for no good reason whatsoever?"

She didn't want to meet his eyes. Couldn't stand the thought of seeing the disbelief there. But there was an ounce of hope, too. Would he have prayed over her like that if he thought she was a liar? Thought she was a criminal?

"That's basically what happened," she answered, fully aware of how incredulous the entire tale sounded. If she had the video, she could show him. Prove everything.

He was frowning now. "And when he punched your friend and kicked him while he was down, that was also completely unprovoked?"

Kennedy weighed her words. If she recounted everything, it would mean repeating the horrific slurs the man had thrown at her and Reuben. It would mean reliving the degrading search where he pressed his body against hers before Reuben jumped between them.

What would her dad tell her to do? There wasn't time for him to get in touch with the trooper he knew. She had to make her decision now.

"I guess that's not the entire story," she admitted. The peace, the strength she'd experienced while Dominic prayed vanished like a flame flaring up on a glass cell spreader drenched in ethanol. The welcomed sense of security that had burned so hot just seconds ago disappeared, leaving behind nothing but cold uncertainty.

Was it the right choice? She didn't know. But it was too late to change her mind.

Kennedy told the officer everything.

CHAPTER 5

Dominic's prayer had disarmed her. Put her in a vulnerable position until she divulged the whole story. She still wasn't sure it was the right thing to do, but at least she got through her recitation calmly. No more choking heaves or suffocating sobs.

When she finished, she searched his face for any telltale signs of anger or disbelief. Had she done it? Had she broken the unwritten code of police procedures and exposed a bad cop?

Would he say the whole thing was her fault, that she or Reuben instigated the confrontation? Would he even believe her?

Dominic was tugging at his short beard hairs. "And you say when the fight was all said and done, the cop who attacked you was gone? Just like that?"

"Yeah." Her voice was weak. What time was it? Exhaustion clung to her individual muscle fibers.

"He didn't stay and write you a ticket? Didn't arrest you

for assault? Nothing?"

She stared at her empty bottle of water and shook her head, realizing how ridiculous the whole thing sounded now that she'd heard it herself. She sat and waited. Waited for him to tell her how stupid she'd been to antagonize an officer. For Dominic to poke a dozen more holes into her story until even she doubted its veracity.

"There's no way an officer would just drive away from a situation like that. Not unless he knew he was guilty and hoped to pretend it never happened."

Kennedy was too busy imagining the conversation she'd have with her dad from a jail cell to piece together the meaning of Dominic's words.

"If he had just cause, he would have written you up. Hauled you both in. That would be the end of it."

For the slightest moment, a spark of hope flickered in Kennedy's core. Was he saying he believed her?

"But instead, he ran away." Dominic was musing now, apparently speaking more to himself than Kennedy. "Which only goes to show he was the guilty party." He leaned forward. "And you didn't get his name?"

"No."

"Didn't see his badge or anything?"

"No."

Frankly, she had been too busy trying to keep him from murdering her best friend to worry about minute details like that.

"Can you at least remember what he looked like?"

Kennedy sighed. She could picture his face but didn't know how to portray it. She did the best she could, certain by Dominic's expression she wasn't helping.

"That could be half the police force you just described there."

"That's what I thought."

He sat for a moment in silence before leveling his gaze. "You know this isn't going to paint a pretty picture when it all comes out in the wash."

What did he mean? Not a pretty picture for the officer involved? Or not pretty for her and Reuben? Kennedy wasn't sure. She glanced up at the walls. There were no clocks here, but she guessed it had to be at least nine by now. The musical would probably be finishing up in the next half hour or so.

She had hoped tonight would end so differently.

She had been looking forward to her date with Reuben for nearly the whole semester. Finally, she'd stopped kidding around like a little junior high girl and admitted her true feelings to herself. Reuben meant so much to her. So much.

She let out her breath. "What happens now?"

She wished Dominic would smile. There was something comforting about his face when he did. But his features were set in a scowl as he tugged on his beard. "I can't tell you what to do, but I can at least spell out your options. You can write a report. File a complaint. If you go that route, I'll show you the ropes. Tell you the right people to meet with. You don't want to walk into the main department building and talk to the first person you see." He let out a sigh that seemed to hold the heaviness of several lifetimes in its breath. "I need to warn you, though, it might not go very far. You didn't get his name. Think you could identify him if you saw him again?"

"Probably."

"Yeah, well, the chances of the chief ordering a dozen of his men to stand in a line-up isn't looking all that hot."

"So there's nothing we can do?" It was such a relief that they were talking about bringing the unruly officer to justice instead of discussing Kennedy and Reuben's plea bargain for assaulting a cop. Part of her would be happy to just walk away and pretend none of this ever happened. She realized, though, that's exactly what Bow Legs was counting on.

So then what? Make herself into an Atticus Finch, stare injustice in the face and jump into some sort of legal battle that was doomed from its inception? And what kind of legal battle would it be if the police department decided to block justice?

Dominic frowned. "I'm not saying it's impossible. I'm just saying you'll face a lot of obstacles along the way. Cops have this code …"

Kennedy rolled her eyes. "I know." She was sick of hearing about it.

"I'm not saying it's right," Dominic inserted. "I'm just saying that's the way it is. Most folks in the department will tell you police brutality doesn't exist, that anyone who finds himself on the wrong end of a nightstick must have been asking for it."

His chest expanded visibly as he inhaled. "This isn't going to be easy."

She couldn't fully comprehend what he meant, but she sensed the warning behind his words. "Well, what would happen if we just let it drop?"

Her question must have pulled Dominic out of some sort of daydream. He shot up his gaze. "Let it drop? You mean don't report it?" He shrugged. "Nothing. Nothing at all would happen. And then next time that same cop pulls over someone he doesn't like or who looks a little funny to him, well, who knows what would happen then? All because of a little bit of nothing."

"But you just said we couldn't make any progress on a case like this." She felt like Milo in *The Phantom Tollbooth*, who agreed to move a pile of sand with a pair of tweezers before realizing how many thousands of years it would actually take him.

"No, it might not turn out in your favor," Dominic replied. "But it's a start. There'd be documentation. If enough reports come in with similar complaints, eventually the department would have to take a good, honest look at itself. And I'm guessing the chief wouldn't like what he'd see."

Kennedy squeezed her eyes shut and massaged her throbbing temples.

"I'm sorry." Dominic stood. "I'm throwing a lot at you right off the bat. I know you've had a hard night."

Kennedy didn't bother coming up with a response. All she wanted was to get home.

Dominic held open the door. "Listen, I'm not gonna keep you here any longer. You think about what I said." He glanced up and down the hall and lowered his voice. "Then when you've made up your mind, let me know how you want to proceed. Like I told you, I can get you in touch with the right people. It's not ..." He took a deep breath before continuing. "The department's not perfect. We do a lot of good. A *lot* of good. But you get one bad apple in there and ..." His voice tapered off. "What I'm trying to say is you have a question, you have a problem, you come to me. I'll help walk you through the steps if you decide to file a grievance, ok?"

Kennedy nodded. For some reason, his kindness toward her made her miss her parents more than normal. Pangs of homesickness pulsed between her firing temples. She swallowed. "Thanks for everything. I really appreciate it." She was too tired to elaborate, but she hoped he knew she was thanking him for more than just his practical assistance. "I think I'll go check on Reuben now. Do you know what room he's in?"

"Just down this hall." Dominic pointed. "I'll walk you there."

"Thanks again."

His smile was both comforting and warm. "That's what we're here for. Follow me. I'll show you the way to your friend."

CHAPTER 6

Reuben's room was nothing more than a ten-by-ten square partitioned off with colorfully patterned curtains. A nurse was handing him a piece of paper. Kennedy entered, uncertain how he would react when he saw her there. "Can I come in?" She hated feeling so uneasy. This was Reuben. She'd never been self-conscious around him before.

The nurse glanced up, apparently oblivious to Kennedy's discomfort. Her face broke into a welcoming grin. "Looks like you have a visitor."

Reuben gave Kennedy a faint smile. "Hey."

"Hey."

The nurse handed him a pen. "If you don't have any more questions, I just need you to sign your discharge papers and you're free to go."

"Leaving already?" Kennedy asked. "That's great. I'll drive you home." She held her breath, half expecting Reuben to decline her invitation.

Instead, he offered her that same tired smile and nodded. "That sounds great. Thanks so much for coming."

The anxiety that had clenched its talons into her spine melted away like dross. A few minutes later, they were back in Willow's car and pulling out of the Providence parking lot.

"How does your head feel?" she asked.

"I'm ok. Just tired."

They rolled along without talking. Kennedy wondered if she should tell him about her meeting with Dominic. What would he think? What would he say?

"I'm really sorry about what happened. That officer ..."

"Forget about it." Reuben turned down the radio, which was set to Willow's favorite classic rock station.

Kennedy drove past looming business complexes and darkened side streets. "It's too bad about *Aida*. I really wanted to see it with you." She stole a quick glance at him. Did he remember how this evening started?

"That's life for you." Reuben stared out his window.

Kennedy recognized the song faintly playing on the radio but didn't know it well enough to make out the words. "Did the doctor say anything? Anything about your injuries?"

"I needed a few stitches. That's all. It's hardly worth mentioning."

Kennedy sensed he was talking about more than just the ER. She let her mind drift off. She had to figure out what to do next. Part of her wanted to file a complaint with the police department. Even if they didn't catch the cop this time, maybe it would force them to make improvements in the future. Then again, if Reuben refused to talk about what happened tonight when it was just the two of them, how could she expect him to come forward and make the complaint with her? Would they both have to testify against Bow Legs, or could she proceed without forcing Reuben to get involved?

She had no idea what he was going through. No idea what he had felt while pressed down against the hood of that car with his hands cuffed behind his back. No idea how much fear, how much anger must have built up in his system before he finally stood up to the cop. She had spent so many late nights with him, shared so many meals in the student union, so many hours in the chemistry lab. He wasn't the type to bottle up negative emotions. She'd never seen him lash out. Never heard him yell. Never seen him angry.

Until tonight.

Now, with him so silent beside her, she wondered how well she actually knew him. When they weren't talking about their studies or arguing over a piece of literature, he would ask all kinds of questions about Kennedy's life. Listen to her stories about growing up in Yanji. Find out every detail he could about her parents. He knew so much about her past. What did she know about his? He had seven sisters, a whole gaggle of nieces and nephews, and an extended family that could fill an entire floor of a New York hotel. But how useful was that information? She didn't know what he was afraid of, didn't know what made him mad, didn't know what struggles he'd overcome. He grew up in a Christian family, talked about going to church on Christmas Eve with his relatives, but he hardly ever mentioned God. She'd spent the past semester and a half feeling so close to him, but the more she thought about it, the more she wondered if she knew him at all.

Another song came on the radio. *Rocket Man* by Elton John. It only reminded her how disappointed she was to miss tonight's musical. Only reminded her how you can be half a foot away from someone you care about, maybe even love, yet still find yourself drowning in an ocean of isolation.

The song invited her to wallow in the homesickness and loneliness that had plagued her since she first arrived at Harvard. A lump lodged itself in the back of her throat, but as comforting as it might be to lose herself in tears, she knew she wouldn't. Not now. Not here. Not with Reuben's elbow just a couple inches from hers.

She thought back on her meeting with Dominic, how a perfect stranger had seen and even soothed her tears. And now here she was with Reuben, her best friend, and her eyes were as dry as anhydrous sodium sulfate.

"I'm sorry." Reuben's voice was faint. At first, she wasn't sure if she heard it at all. "With the paramedics. When I yelled at you."

She turned the song off. "It's ok."

"No, I was acting like a jerk. I'm sorry."

"I forgive you," she whispered. Did that mean they could talk now? Did that mean their encounter with Bow Legs was no longer taboo?

"I was …" He sucked in his breath. "I was really scared."

She nodded, mistrustful of her voice.

"I was afraid he was going to hurt you, and I'd have to stand by and watch."

She bit her lip, wondering how different things might have turned out if Reuben hadn't intervened. Maybe nothing would have happened. Nothing at all. The cop could have sent them away with a warning. Or he might have taken them in until Kennedy could prove the stuff in the Ziploc was tea leaves like she claimed. Wasn't it Aslan in *Prince Caspian* who said you don't get to know the what-ifs?

What if they hadn't been pulled over? What if they'd gone to see *Aida* like they planned? What if Reuben had told her afterwards the secret he'd been meaning to share?

"They talked to you at the hospital, didn't they?" Reuben was always soft-spoken, and this time Kennedy had to strain to make out his words.

"Yeah. I didn't really have much of a choice."

"Well, I'm just glad it's over."

She didn't want to tell him it might not be over like he expected. Didn't want to tell him she was considering filing a complaint.

She tested her voice. "Hey, can I ask you a question?" Even with her eyes focused on the road, she sensed his whole body tense.

"What is it?"

She tried to make her words sound natural. Unassuming. "Why didn't you tell the policeman at the hospital what happened?"

He let out his breath, almost as if he were relieved. "Back home, nothing good ever comes from dealing with the police. They're all corrupt, and they don't even try to hide it. So when we got pulled over, I kept reminding myself things were different in America. But they weren't."

Kennedy could empathize. If it hadn't been for Dominic and his prayer, she probably would feel mistrustful of everyone in a blue uniform at this point, too.

"And I haven't been here long, but I've seen enough to know how it would turn out. Everyone who heard about what happened to us would turn it into a race issue. It wouldn't be about a bad policeman abusing his power. It wouldn't be about a sexist policeman taking advantage of a college girl. It would be about a white policeman pulling over a black man. That's all anybody would see."

Maybe he was right, but Kennedy didn't understand why that would make him reluctant to bring the officer to justice. "So you think a white cop should be able to harass a black man and get away with it?"

"I don't think any cop should be able to harass any person and get away with it."

"You're not making sense."

Reuben shrugged. "It's hard to explain. But I still don't want you to make a big deal about it. Let's just forget it."

Kennedy tried not to show her frustration. "So why else did you refuse to talk to the police?" There had to be more reasons than his counter-intuitive argument.

"I'm not comfortable with it, ok?" He must have sensed he was being more forceful than necessary. "I'm sorry. There are just some things I don't feel like talking about."

She furrowed her brows. "I thought we could talk about everything."

"No." His voice was weighed down with so much heaviness, so much sadness that Kennedy held her tongue.

"No," he repeated. "Not everything."

CHAPTER 7

Kennedy dropped Reuben off near his side of campus after making plans to meet the next morning for a late breakfast. Her legs were heavy as she trudged from the parking lot to her dorm. She wondered why some people tried to cheer up their friends by reminding them of how much worse things could be. Of course things could be worse. She could be in a holding cell while cops ran tests on her roommate's bag of loose-leaf tea. She could be standing outside a morgue waiting to identify Reuben's body. She could be bleeding to death in the back of some deserted alley where the policeman dragged her and raped her. Maybe he didn't work for the police department at all. Maybe he stole a car and a cop uniform and drove around town looking for prey.

Of course things could be worse. But how was that supposed to make her feel better?

The door to her room was slightly ajar as she made her way down the hall. She swung it open, ready to let her brain drop into the sweet bliss of dreamless sleep. Sinking down on her bed, she kicked off her shoes. Willow was staring at her computer screen, probably playing one of those shooter video games she liked so much. For being a pacifist, she really enjoyed virtual violence. Kennedy wasn't even sure her roommate noticed her walk in.

"Thanks for letting me use your car." She took the keys out of her pocket and tossed them on Willow's desk.

She didn't look up.

"What are you doing?" Kennedy asked.

"Oh, nothing much. Just watching this little video of you beating up a cop."

Kennedy sprang out of bed. Hovered behind Willow's shoulder to stare at the monitor. "What are you talking about?"

"I got a visit from the police department. They asked what I knew about this video a commuter took of some altercation between a cop, a black man, and white woman. I told them I had no clue what they were talking about, so they said they identified my car by the plates. The same car you and your little platonic boyfriend took out tonight. How was the musical, by the way? Was it good?"

"We didn't see it." As much as she wanted to, Kennedy couldn't pry her eyes away from the screen. The video was running on some kind of loop. It started when the policeman kicked Reuben and ended with Kennedy jumping on his back.

"Interesting stuff, isn't it?" Willow cocked her head to the side and then punched her monitor off. "I already made you a cup of tea. You gonna tell me what happened?"

Kennedy slunk down on her roommate's jumbo beanbag. Willow swiveled her chair around to face her and passed her an oversized mug.

"We got pulled over on the way to the show." As Kennedy filled in the details, she wondered how many more times she'd have to recount this story before she could move on. Somewhere in the back of her mind was the nagging suspicion that normal pre-med students didn't go through this sort of stuff. Normal pre-med students didn't get harassed by police officers on the side of the road.

Willow was silent while Kennedy talked. As soon as she finished, Kennedy expected her to go on some tirade about police brutality and black oppression and the failed justice system in the United States. Instead, she reached over and squeezed Kennedy's hand. "I'm really sorry you had to go through all that. It must have been awful."

Kennedy sniffed into her mug. "Yeah."

"Well, I've got the name of the policeman who stopped by.

He was kind of hot, actually, if you're into the trim, athletic, middle-aged type." She pulled a business card out of her pocket. "Here's his information. I was going to invite him to stay and wait for you, but I wanted to get the juicy details first before I passed on his message."

Kennedy stared at the name on the card. Great. Another cop she'd never heard of. Another officer who might be just as bad as Bow Legs, perhaps worse.

"I didn't give him your name or anything, by the way." Willow ran her fingers through her hair. She had cut it short over Christmas break and dyed it just a few weeks ago, so now it was brunette with purple tips. When she was going out, she wore it spiked and gelled, but tonight it hung loose, framing her face like a heart. "I mean, it's none of my business why a cop was giving you a piggyback ride, but I figured if you didn't want to be named, I wasn't going to narc on you. I just told him I've got several friends I let borrow my car, and I wasn't sure whose turn it was to take it out tonight."

"Thanks," Kennedy muttered. Her mind was reeling. So someone had a video. It was short, but the cop's face was clear. Would that be enough evidence to convict him?

Willow pouted her lips. "So, what are you gonna do? You gonna call up Mr. Mid-Life Crisis and cry the whole story into his hard, chiseled shoulder?"

Kennedy stared at her lap. "Reuben doesn't want me to make a big deal out of it. I think he just wants to pretend it never happened."

Willow gestured to her monitor. "It's already on Channel 2. White cop and black kid? It's not the kind of story that goes away."

The more they talked, the more Kennedy began to understand Reuben's line of reasoning. Everyone, even Willow, was doing the same thing. Turning it into another instance of white versus black. What about Kennedy? What about all the cop's chauvinist remarks? His roaming hands? Was it ok to be a sexist pervert as long as you were abusing women of your own race? She was sick of it all. Maybe Reuben had the right idea. Shut the door and pray it'd all disappear.

"I don't know," Kennedy sighed. She knew what Willow and all the other students in Professor Hill's class would do. March their story in front of every reporter, every news outlet available. Keep shouting until someone listened. Until someone demanded the Boston Police Department make the changes that needed to be made. Until they weeded out Officer Bow Legs and any other corrupt cronies like him.

Kennedy understood the thirst for justice. But there was also a need for healing. For privacy. Every time she watched the four-second video on Willow's computer screen, she relived that humiliating attack all over again. Did she have the fortitude to let journalists and politicians and civil rights activists prod through her wounds before the blood even had time to coagulate?

Willow propped her feet up on her bed. "Well, it's not gonna take the journalists too long to identify you from that video. And you better be ready, because these police brutality cases are all the same. It's a media frenzy where everyone sees who can be first to crucify the victim. Like that black kid the cop shot in the back. Died instantly. And guess what? While the black folks held vigil for justice, the white police force and their media buddies were digging up all the dirt they could find to prove the boy had it coming. Even though he was unarmed. Even though several witnesses claimed he wasn't resisting arrest. But as soon as the media comes out to show this boy was a 'troubled youth,' everyone forgets about justice and just assumes a black kid with a few petty crimes in his record deserves to be executed point-blank. That's America for you. Land of the stinking free."

Somewhere in the pit of her gut, Kennedy wondered if her roommate might be right. Would the media try to attack Reuben? Is that why he wanted to remain so secretive? Is that why he begged her to keep the story from the police and the press? He was such a mature, responsible young man. Was it possible he had anything to hide? Or was growing up in Kenya with its corrupt police system enough to make him paranoid of anyone in a uniform?

"You want some more tea?" Willow held up her electric kettle.

"No, thanks."

"What are you going to do?"

"I don't know. Right now, I just want to rest."

Willow gave an encouraging half-smile. "I don't blame you. Just let me know if you need anything, ok?"

How about a time machine like what the H. G. Wells inventor made? If she could only start today over. Take the T to the Opera House instead of borrowing Willow's car. Or drive another route, where her path would have never crossed Bow Legs to begin with.

She slipped into bed, clothes and all, and pulled the covers over her head. Things could have turned out worse, she reminded herself. But then again, they could have turned out so much better.

CHAPTER 8

She should have known she'd never be able to fall asleep on a night like this. By eleven o'clock, she'd checked half a dozen times to see if Channel 2 had any breaking news. The story was still running at the top of their website, along with the short clip of Kennedy jumping on the policeman's back while he pummeled Reuben.

Other outlets had picked up the piece, too. The story was trending all over the internet. Black leaders were already calling for the police department to divulge the name and rank of the officer, citing how suspicious it was that he hadn't made any arrests and was entirely unavailable for comment. The police department hadn't released any official statements either, but someone close to the head office hinted that the chief was doing everything in the scope of his authority to figure out the whole truth. The chief also urged anyone to call in with information about the two "suspects," as she and Reuben were called in certain publications, while others referred to them as victims.

She kept reloading one webpage after another before she finally flipped on her lamp. Willow was still awake at her desk, the ear buds and flashing lights from the screen proof she had moved back to her blood and gore video games.

Kennedy still hadn't decided what she should do. Willow was probably right. If she told the police who she was, gave her side of the story, they'd try to find a way to make the public believe this whole mess was her fault. But if she stayed silent, what would stop the same thing from happening to victims all up and down Boston? Could she feel safe knowing that cops like Bow Legs were out on patrol?

And what about the race issue? The journalists all treated this as a black and white incident, nothing more and nothing less. On the one hand, she was glad there were watchdog groups ready to protect the rights of minorities, but she still couldn't shake the feeling that pegging her encounter with Bow Legs as simply a race incident was akin to forcing a triangular stopper into a round lab beaker. Sure, she could cite the slurs Bow Legs spurted out like venom, but he'd called her as many bad names as Reuben. There was more to it than ugly racism — misogyny, bigotry, power hunger for starters.

She had to do something. But what? If she went to the police now, what would that mean for her and Reuben? Would they be forced to relive their inhumane treatment each time they attempted to prove that the wrongs they suffered really happened? Was it worth subjecting themselves to public scrutiny until their past secrets and public records were exposed for all to see? Was she ready to accept that cost? Was she willing to force Reuben to do the same?

But the police must already know about her and Reuben. Wasn't that why they sent Dominic to the hospital? So why did they waste their energy asking the public to help identify them?

Unless Dominic had kept their identities a secret. Could he do that? Would he?

Then there was Ian. Kennedy had run into the redheaded journalist a time or two last semester during the peak of her fifteen minutes in the public eye. She had no reason to doubt him, but that certainly wasn't grounds to trust somebody, either. Didn't most journalists scurry around trying to break their story first? Was he just waiting for the hype to increase a little more before he told the world who Kennedy really was?

Would he do that to her? Or maybe the better question was why wouldn't he?

This was all too much for Kennedy. She didn't know about police proceedings other than the tidbits she'd gleaned here and there from the cop dramas she watched with her dad. Besides that and an occasional suspense or detective novel, Kennedy had no idea what she was getting into. She had always assumed that in America, if you were a conscientious citizen and minded your own business, the police would have no reason to bother you. It was like health insurance, important to have around but as long as you were healthy and took care of yourself, and maybe with a little bit of luck, you didn't expect to need it.

Now here she was, wondering if she turned herself in to the police if they'd hail her as a hero for exposing a bad cop or if they'd arrest her for assaulting an officer. How would she know what would happen until she made the first move? And if she waited for them to find her — which they could do easily if they really wanted to — would she look guiltier than she would have if she came forth voluntarily?

"You awake?" Willow asked, taking off her headset. "Sorry. I was trying to be quiet."

"It wasn't you."

"Just having a hard time sleeping?"

"Yeah."

Willow gave Kennedy an almost maternal smile. "Well, you'll be happy to know that Gordon Clarence has taken an interest in your video."

"Who?" The name sounded familiar, but Kennedy couldn't place it.

"Gordon Clarence. The reverend. Head and founder of the Black Fraternity?"

Kennedy groaned. She had read some of his speeches in Professor Hill's class. The last person she wanted championing her case was someone like him.

Willow clicked her mouse. "Here, listen to this. This is Gordon Clarence in a video address to his congregation about the piggyback attack. That's what they're calling what happened. Cute, huh?" She glanced at Kennedy's face and then ducked back behind her screen. "Anyway, here's part of the speech." She unplugged her ear buds, and a booming, rhythmic voice filled the room. *"And that's why I'm asking you tonight, brothers and sisters, that's why I'm standing here before you wanting to know when will the world see these cops for what they really are — a militarized force intent on occupying the neighborhoods and communities where our brothers and sisters are trying to make a peaceful life for themselves. When will the mayor and people of Boston stand up to defend our brother and sister who were brutalized in full daylight by an officer who clearly sees no value in the lives of black men and women? When will my brothers and sisters of color rise up and declare with one voice, 'Enough. Enough of the victimization of our women and children. Enough of the ...'"*

A knock on the door interrupted the reverend's tirade. Willow paused the recording, and both girls glanced nervously at each other.

"You expecting anyone?" Kennedy asked.

Willow shook her head.

Kennedy wished their doors had little peep holes like in hotel rooms. What if it was the police? What if they'd come to arrest her or bring her in for questioning? It was a good thing she hadn't gotten into her pajamas.

Willow stood up and was arranging her purple-tipped hair. "I'll get it. You just ..." She glanced at Kennedy's bed as if she might find a hiding place. "You just wait there."

She cracked the door open. "Yes?"

"I'm here with the Boston Police Department."

Willow adjusted her position so she blocked the policeman's view into the room. "I already answered a few questions earlier. Is there something else you fellows needed?" Her foot was planted by the door, keeping him from opening it any farther.

Kennedy's heart pounded. Her mouth was dry. If they took her in to the station, would they let her make an international call? She would do anything to be back in Yanji with her parents. Anywhere but here.

"I actually stopped by to check on Kennedy. Is she in?"

There was something familiar about his voice. Kennedy tried to peek around her roommate to get a look at his face.

"Kennedy? She likes to stay out late. She sometimes doesn't come back until ..."

The policeman nudged the door slightly and pointed. "Isn't that her in the bed?"

Willow let out a casual laugh. "Oh, yeah, but you know, she's been asleep. Came home right after her afternoon classes and just crashed ..."

The door was wide open now, but the officer didn't step in. He gave Kennedy an apologetic smile. "Hi, Kennedy."

She let out her breath. "Hi, Dominic."

Willow turned around, raised one of her penciled eyebrows at Kennedy, and then gave a little shrug.

"Can I come in?" he asked. "Or would you rather talk out here?"

Willow was slipping on a colorful shawl. "You know what? I completely spaced out and forgot that our director called a rehearsal tonight. I'm already late, so I better run.

Don't wait up for me," she called as she hurried out the door. Dominic and Kennedy watched her leave in a wave of colors and patterns.

"That's your roommate?" he asked.

Kennedy nodded. "That's Willow. You can come in," she told him when she realized he was still standing on the threshold of her room.

"I'm sorry to bother you like this." He looked around awkwardly until Kennedy pointed him to Willow's swivel desk chair. "I'm glad I found you awake. You doing ok?"

She shrugged. "I guess." She couldn't read him. Was he here on official police business? More questions, maybe? Or was this some sort of social call? She wanted to trust him. Desperately wanted to trust him. With her dad so far away, who else was there to help her navigate through this mess of legal proceedings she'd gotten herself dumped into? But just because Dominic was a Christian, did that mean he was safe to talk to? Just because his prayer had covered her with a peace and tranquility she hadn't experienced in years, maybe in her entire life, did that mean he wouldn't betray her?

He scratched his cheek. "So, I guess maybe you heard about the news reports." It came out as half question, half statement.

She nodded.

"And well, the chief, he's doing what he can to save face. Trying to avoid any sort of scandal."

It made sense. That seemed like the sort of thing a chief of police would do after a video leaked of one of his officers kicking an innocent man.

"We know the officer in question. Got that figured out even before we saw the tape based on your interview and the location of the engagement."

Engagement. He was using the same terminology as the characters in Willow's computer games. Another reminder that, as kind as he appeared, he was still one of them. Part of the same force as the man who'd landed Reuben in the hospital. Who'd groped Kennedy along a busy Boston highway.

"And obviously, we had your name right away too, but we're keeping that from the press right now for several reasons." His shoulders rose as he took in a noisy inhale. "I just got back from talking with your friend. With Reuben."

Kennedy tried not to let him see how nervous she was when he said Reuben's name. She clenched her teeth shut to keep from spewing out the dozens of questions streaming through her consciousness.

"And after talking with him, I'm even more convinced about what I'm going to say."

Kennedy squinted slightly. Studying his face. If she were a card player, she'd have a better feel for whether or not he was bluffing.

"I know at the hospital I said some good could come out of making a complaint. Might not happen right away, might not result in immediate progress, but if you were willing to jump through the fire, I told you I'd help you start that ball rolling."

She tested his speech, mulling over each phrase. Like one of Willow's gluten-free, sugar-free, chia seed muffins, his words looked appealing at first glance. Looked like words spoken by a friend. A confidante. But the more she analyzed them, the more mistrustful she grew.

He clasped his hands on his knees. "Now that I've seen the way the department's scurrying to handle this particular PR mess, I'm not convinced that coming forward right now is going to be in your best interest. Or your friend's." He put special emphasis on that last part, so much so that it came out sounding like a threat.

She didn't know what to say. She wished Willow were here. Anyone she knew. Anyone she could trust.

"Listen, I know I'm contradicting everything I told you earlier, and you gotta believe me, it's eating me up inside. But not everyone's called to be a David. And you don't want to make the same mistake as others and underestimate Goliath, either."

Kennedy's headache had eased up when she was resting in bed but now returned with even more cruelty. What *others* was he talking about?

He spread his hands out. "I know I'm being cryptic, and part of that's because I'm in a delicate situation myself."

She didn't care about his delicate situation, about his David and Goliath metaphors or anything else he was talking about. She didn't even care so much about vengeance as she cared about people believing her side of the story. What happened to her was wrong. If the chief of police called her on the phone, told her he believed every word she said, and asked her to accept his apology, Kennedy could live with that.

Almost.

It would sure beat sitting here listening to Dominic pretend to care about her and her feelings while trying at the same time to convince her to shut up and accept tonight's harassment as a normal East Coast occurrence.

She wouldn't. She couldn't.

"So here's what's happened so far," he continued. "The chief has a press release set to deliver first thing Friday morning. He's going to explain how one of our cops pulled two people over for speeding. During their encounter, he had enough evidence to suspect the couple of drug possession."

"That's ridiculous." Kennedy couldn't keep the edge out of her voice. "He didn't even have a reason to pull us over in the first place. It was rush hour. I couldn't have been speeding if I wanted to."

Dominic nodded. "I know that." Kennedy couldn't figure out if that should make her feel relieved or even angrier now that he was telling her to give up any hope for justice.

"At that point the chief is going to admit our man made a mistake."

"Good."

Dominic held up his hand before Kennedy could say anything else. "The mistake was that even though he had suspected you of drug possession, he failed to call for backup. And if you hear the chief's side of the story, he's going to be all over it as an example of how the city needs to put more resources into the police force. The reason our man didn't call for backup, at least as the public is going to hear it tomorrow morning, is because we're short-staffed. Budget cuts, lay-offs, the whole enchilada."

"But he attacked us."

Dominic shrugged. "The chief already got the public believing you two are druggies at this point. And based on that video I saw, he won't have a hard time arguing you assaulted him first. There's a reason it's being called the piggyback attack, you know."

Rage boiled in Kennedy's brain, making it impossible to put any rational thought into a cohesive sentence.

The worst part about this whole encounter was how shaken up Dominic was pretending to be over it all. "That's what I mean when I'm telling you not to underestimate Goliath."

"He grabbed me." Kennedy blinked back tears, no longer of shame or fear but of blind fury. "He had his hands all over me." She shut her eyes so she wouldn't have to watch Dominic shrug another time.

"Cops search suspects. It's what they do." Did Dominic really believe any of this? Did he really believe she and Reuben were drug pushers?

"You can search the baggie. All it had was tea."

Dominic frowned. "Do you have any idea how many drug busts we see a week? How hard do you think it would be for someone in the force to sprinkle your roommate's tea leaves with a little weed, huh?"

"They can't do that." Kennedy hadn't realized how

childish her argument sounded until she heard it come out of her mouth.

"But they do. It's not right. I'm not making any excuses. That cop, based on what you told me at Providence, he had no business pulling you over, making you get out of the car, restraining your friend, none of it. But it doesn't matter what I think. What matters is what the chief thinks, and all he's thinking about is how he's gonna protect his own. It's an unwritten code."

Unwritten code. That phrase was like fingernails on a chalkboard. So this was it? This was the Goliath she had dreamed of going up against? What chance did she have?

She would never look at a policeman the same way again.

There had to be some other option. This was America. It wasn't China or Kenya or some other country riddled with corruption.

Things like this didn't happen here.

Did they?

A memory tugged at the back of her brain. Something Pastor Carl said in one of his recent sermons. A Bible verse from Proverbs. Or was it Psalms? A verse about God bringing justice to light like the noonday sun. A verse about Christians waiting patiently for God's truth to prevail.

But why should she have to wait for it? She wanted it now. Everything Dominic said made sense. Of course, that's how the chief would slant the issue — an officer going about his business, risking his life to make the streets of Boston safer, when all of a sudden he's attacked by two suspects, and the force is so overworked and underpaid that he fails to call for backup. It was a flawlessly logical argument, however wrong it was. Like a bilayer of phospholipids surrounding a cell's organelles — perfectly watertight.

How could she stand against a Goliath like this?

The truth was she couldn't.

"Wait a minute." A seed of doubt had germinated in Kennedy's mind. It was taking root now. Sprouting. "If he was so convinced we were criminals, why did he just drive off? Why did he leave Reuben there bleeding on the pavement?"

She had him now. This was her slingshot. This was how she'd defeat the Philistine giant.

Dominic's frown did nothing to bolster her newfound encouragement. "The PR guys already thought of that. Between you and me, the fact that he did run off is the only reason the chief hasn't pulled you both in and arrested you for assaulting an officer. He won't admit it, not even to us, but we can all sniff out a rotten egg. If our man believed half of what the chief's saying — that you were carrying drugs or attacked him unprovoked or anything like that — he would have thrown every citation in the book at you. But he didn't. He ran off, and I'm speaking strictly off the record here, but that's the biggest reason I believed your story to begin with." His expression softened for a moment.

She was too busy formulating her next argument to let his words sink in. "But that means that we can't have really done all those things, or else he wouldn't have just left us there like that. So there must be some way to prove to the public ..."

"You're not understanding something here," Dominic interrupted. "The chief doesn't want the public to know the truth. He doesn't want the protesters, the marchers, the Gordon Clarences all taking to our streets. He'd rather throw the media a bone and bury the truth in the backyard. I'm not saying it's right. I'm just saying it's the way things are done."

"So that's all?" She hadn't meant to sound so accusatory. She just couldn't understand how someone like Dominic, someone with a powerful faith who obviously loved the Lord, could sit there and tell her that lies and gross abuses of justice were normal, just as much a part of Boston life as the swan boats in the Common or a strong nor'easter in the winter. Kennedy refused to believe it. "Can't you do something?"

"I am doing something." He pointed to his badge. "I'm getting up every day, begging God to make me a salt and a light to those other officers. I'm putting on this uniform. I'm not the kind of guy who rolls over and watches corruption. Not usually. So when I say it's time to let it go, I really mean it. If not for your own sake, at least for your friend's."

The mention of Reuben was enough to make Kennedy's whole body tense. "What do you mean?"

"I told you I saw Reuben earlier. He has his reasons — very personal reasons — for keeping this quiet. Let me tell you how the chief sees it. You two stay out of the public eye, don't come forward, we keep your identity secret ..." He held up his hand to stop Kennedy from interrupting. "We keep your identity secret," he repeated, "and we don't charge you with assault or possession."

He leaned forward in Willow's chair as if he were about to stand up. "But if you go to the press, if you start broadcasting your side of the story ..." He shook his head. "The chief is willing to do whatever it takes to keep his own guy covered. I need you to remember that. You shout police brutality, I guarantee you they'll find marijuana in that tea-leaf baggie, no matter what was in it when he took it out of your car. You accuse his guy, the chief accuses you. Not just possession. Not just battery. But your past, too. Any mistake you ever made, any …"

"I don't have anything to hide." She sounded braver than she felt.

Dominic stood. "Maybe not. But what if Reuben does? Out of respect for him, and because I gave him my word, that's all I'm gonna say. But if he's your friend like you claim, you really should let this case drop."

His shoulders sagged as he opened the door. "I'm sorry." He let himself out. As he pulled the door shut behind him, he looked back once and added, "I really, really wanted tonight to end differently for you."

Kennedy didn't reply. She was feeling the exact same thing.

CHAPTER 9

Kennedy had just finished brushing her teeth when Willow barged into their room. "You decent?" she called out. "I brought a friend with me." She led in a tall student Kennedy recognized from Willow's theater troupe.

She tried not to groan. It was almost midnight. What was Willow thinking?

"I'm really tired." Kennedy reached over to turn her desk lamp off. "Could you two go somewhere else to hang out?"

Willow tossed her bag onto her desk. "Oh, we're not here for that." She put her hand on his shoulder. "I couldn't get Othello to go to bed with me even if I wanted to."

Kennedy was left wondering what was so humorous. "Your name's really Othello?" she asked, but the two of them were too busy chuckling to answer.

"So anyway ..." Willow plopped down in her purple bean bag chair, and Othello sank in beside her. He crossed his leg and draped his arm around her shoulder. All he needed was a beanie cap to look like some sort of African-American beatnik poet.

Willow arched her penciled eyebrows and got that artificial look she adopted whenever she was around her theater friends. "I told Othello about your little encounter tonight, you and your pseudo-boyfriend."

Kennedy was about to ask how much he knew, but as if taking a cue from somewhere offstage, Othello shook his head and muttered, "Now, that's what I'm talking about. It's that sort of warfare, that type of dictatorial oppression that's been plaguing our country since the days of slavery."

He paused for a moment to sigh. It was no wonder he was in the theater department.

"For centuries, my people have been the victims of a coordinated assault, a cultural genocide, not with bombs but with racial profiling. The ghettoization of our homes. The methodical incarceration of our young men. The rape of our women. The abduction of our children by welfare workers backed up by policemen armed with guns who know nothing of our way of life, our culture."

Kennedy didn't know how to answer. It was as if Othello had opened his mouth, and Reverend Clarence came spewing out.

"I just want you to know how grateful we are to you,"

he told her, meeting her eyes for the first time. "Sometimes it takes a tragedy like this for people to pay attention. Black men are brutalized, terrorized every day, and nobody cares. But you, a white woman who gets harassed — now that's something the hypnotized majority of this nation will pay attention to. And I just want to tell you that I'm honored you're here to stand side by side with us to speak out against the racism that's poisoned our schools, polluted our judiciary system, and plagued our inner cities."

He ended his words with a flourish, and Kennedy wondered if he was expecting applause or something of the sort. She'd heard all those arguments before in Reverend Clarence's speeches and Professor Hill's classroom. But this was the first time it'd come addressed directly to her. She wasn't sure if she should give Othello an ovation or apologize to him on behalf of every single white American, past, present, and future.

It couldn't be that bad, could it? And if it was, how would she know? How could she — a white American who'd lived in China since the third grade — know what it was like for minorities in the inner cities? How would she know if it was as bad as Othello said if she'd never seen it, never experienced it firsthand?

From the beanbag chair where Willow was running her fingers through his short curly hair, Othello nodded sagely. "It's hard to find kindred spirits in our light-skinned counterparts."

Kennedy was too tired to tell if he was giving her a compliment or insulting her, but she knew she had to correct his assumptions. "Actually, I haven't decided whether I'm going to file a complaint or not." All she wanted was to go to sleep. She could make up her mind later.

Othello turned to Willow. "You said she was going to take her story to the news outlets."

Willow fidgeted with her scarf. "I said I thought she was going to. There's a big difference."

"I haven't decided yet." Kennedy's voice came out harsher than she intended, but she didn't care.

Othello scowled. "If you keep quiet, it's just as bad as if you let that cop murder your friend. You know that, don't you?"

Willow put her hand on his shoulder. "Hey, all she said was she needed more time to make up her mind. I think it's only fair …"

He wasn't paying any attention. "So you're just like everyone else. You don't care what happens to us. You'll leave it up to the Reverend Clarences of the world to plan their protests and marches, and you'll just sit cozy, swimming in your white privilege ..."

Willow nudged him in the ribs. "I told you to leave her alone."

"Sure." He shrugged. "Sure. The cops are out exterminating our race one traffic stop at a time, but hey, I wouldn't want you two pretty porcelains losing sleep over it or anything."

He could say whatever he wanted. He had no idea what he was talking about. He could harp and rail about police brutality and violence against blacks. She was too tired to listen. Willow followed him out of the room, their ensuing argument loud enough to wake up anybody lucky enough to have fallen asleep already. It didn't matter. Kennedy didn't have the energy to think about it, let alone let his words discourage her.

She just needed rest. Without even bothering to turn off the light, she covered her head with her blanket and squeezed her eyes shut. Her brain soaked up the comfort of her bed like parched roots drinking up rainfall.

Sleep. That's all she wanted to do. Everything would be clearer in the morning.

CHAPTER 10

Kennedy woke up Friday with the sun pouring in through her dorm room window. An uneasy feeling sloshed around in her empty gut. Even her sleep had failed to provide the reprieve she'd hoped for. She wasn't any more rested than she'd been last night.

She glanced at Willow's bed. Empty. Her roommate never woke up early. Did that mean she'd stayed out? Had she spent the night at Othello's?

Kennedy scratched her head, grimacing when she felt how slimy and gross her hair was. She hadn't even taken a shower last night. At least the thought of washing off all of Bow Legs' lingering filth was enough motivation to get her out of bed. As she was gathering her toiletries together, her phone beeped. She glanced at the text message from Willow.

Headed to the protest. Want a ride?

Protest?

Did Kennedy even want to know?

She was tempted to ignore the message and take an

impossibly long shower until her skin was lobster red and her mind washed of all the defiling memories from yesterday. She wasn't due to meet Reuben for breakfast for another hour, and then their only class was children's literature. After that, the weekend. She couldn't remember if she had anything else scheduled, but she wasn't going to worry about that right now.

One day at a time.

Pastor Carl's wife Sandy had once encouraged Kennedy to meditate on the Sermon on the Mount, let the words sink in and minister to her soul. Kennedy was such a speed reader — the only way she could keep up with her courses and still have time to enjoy a few classics or mystery novels on the side — that it was hard for her to slow down to make her Scripture reading very contemplative. As a countermeasure, Sandy encouraged her to memorize certain passages that stood out the most to her, so Kennedy had started with Jesus's admonition to stop worrying about tomorrow.

So far, she was only a couple verses in, but it was a start. This morning though, Kennedy didn't have time to spend in the Bible. She had to clean herself up. She'd pray while she was in the shower. God wouldn't mind, would he?

She grabbed her towel and had just slipped on her germ-proof flip-flops when her phone beeped once more. Willow again, sending nothing but a series of question marks.

Kennedy huffed as she set the shower caddy down on her desk.

Another beep.

Check the news.

Great. This was not the way Kennedy planned on starting her Friday. She typed Channel 2's web address into her browser and was met with a zoomed-in photo of Boston's chief of police who had recently addressed the public. Kennedy scanned the article. It was exactly what Dominic had warned her it would be. The cop she'd met last night — apparently his name was Lorence Burgess and not Bow Legs after all — had a stellar record. He helped crack a murder investigation a few years ago in North End, two men with Mafia connections who dumped a body into a pier before going after a couple of unlucky witnesses. He traveled around to elementary schools warning kids about the dangers of gangs. Kennedy rolled her eyes. He probably baked chocolate chip cookies for his shut-in mama every weekend, too.

After extoling his officer's flawless record, the chief explained that last night at 6:34 pm, Burgess had pulled over two suspects in a drug-related case, which apparently sounded more convincing than the speeding story Dominic had predicted.

Halfway down the screen was a grainy picture of Kennedy

hanging onto Officer Burgess' back. Reuben wasn't in the shot at all. They had cropped that part out, probably because it wouldn't look so good to show Burgess kicking an unarmed black man. At that point, the article quoted the chief regretfully informing the people of Boston that when Burgess was attacked by his two "alleged suspects," there were not enough backup officers on duty. The next several paragraphs dealt with budget cuts on the police force. The article ended, almost like an afterthought, with the notice of a peaceful protest organized by the Reverend Gordon Clarence, who aimed to let the mayor and police department know that the people of Boston wouldn't stand for the slaughter of innocent African-Americans.

Kennedy had lost her appetite by the time she finished reading. She texted Willow back, saying she had to go to her lit class and wouldn't make the gathering. She looked at the clock. Still enough time to shower and dress and maybe catch up on a little reading before she met Reuben at the student union.

She glanced once more at the news article, hoping her brain had made up the entire story, but there was the picture of her straddling Burgess' back. Her only solace was that she hadn't been named. She and Reuben were still safe. They still had their privacy.

For now.

CHAPTER 11

She arrived at the student union a few minutes early and made her way to a table in the back where she and Reuben could enjoy some seclusion. She avoided making eye contact with anyone. Why were they all staring at her? How many of them had seen the video clip? Did they recognize her? She opened her used copy of *My Side of the Mountain* and wondered what it would feel like to run away into the wilderness like Sam Gribley so she could live on her own. Completely alone.

Things had been going so well lately. The panic attacks were finally under control. She had made it through the first half of the semester without any major drama. She was one of the few first-years on campus lucky enough to get along with her roommate. She and Willow had almost nothing in common besides mutual respect, but apparently that was enough for the mismatched pair.

Classes were going well. Even her parents had stopped hovering over her from ten thousand miles away in Yanji.

Her mom didn't cry anymore when they talked on the phone, lamenting that her little girl was so far from home. For a short time, life had been good. Really good. And of course, there was Reuben. Always so kind and encouraging. Such an important part of her first year at Harvard. As excited as she was to go back home to Yanji at the end of the semester, she hated the idea of going all summer without seeing him. She had always imagined romance like what happened to Marius and Cosette in *Les Miserables*, when two people look at each other across the way, their hearts fluttering, and in that moment they both know they were meant for each other. Her relationship with Reuben, by contrast, had grown slowly. Organically. Whatever they had, be it a friendship or something deeper, it had sneaked up on them quietly while neither one was looking. Was it God who'd brought them together? If it was, then why couldn't he have kept them away from Officer Burgess last night? Why couldn't he let them go to *Aida* together, let the music surround them, let the love story enfold them? Who knew what would have happened next?

"To know what would have happened, child?" Kennedy could almost hear Aslan's voice in her head. *"No. Nobody is ever told that."*

She shut her book. No use studying *My Side of the Mountain* when her brain was still stuck in the Narnia world. It was just as well. Reuben was coming toward her wearing a tired smile. His step was slower, too.

"Good morning." She eyed his tray of food.

He slipped into the seat across from her. "Hey. Aren't you eating?"

"I'm not that hungry." Kennedy forced a cheerful tone. "How's your head today?"

He scooped his scrambled eggs up with his fork. She was glad to see him devour his first bite with his usual zeal. "Nothing to worry about." It didn't really answer her question.

She nodded toward her book. "Have you caught up on your reading?"

"I was a little busy last night," he muttered.

Kennedy would have liked to get herself some food, anything to relieve this awkward tension, but she was too nervous to eat. Maybe she should have asked Willow for more information about that protest. What would Dominic think? It wasn't as though she and Reuben had anything to do with it, but would the police suspect they were involved? Would the chief retaliate like Dominic predicted?

There were so many things she wanted to talk to Reuben about. Not just the protest. Not just the visit from Dominic at her dorm where he all but threatened her into silence. There was so much more they needed to discuss. Like Reuben's aloof behavior. Was he angry about what they went through, or was there more to it? What did Dominic mean when he said that Reuben had a secret reason to keep their story from the press? How was Kennedy supposed to react to all this confusion?

"I got a visit from the police last night," Reuben said through a mouthful of sourdough toast.

She lifted her gaze. Tried to read his face. "What did they say?"

"I was so tired, I hardly remember any of it."

Slowly, the tension she had felt between them lifted, like a cloud of condensation slowly dispersing. She eyed the French toast and strawberry sauce on his plate. Maybe she could find her appetite after all. She also found the courage to ask, "Do you think we should tell someone what happened? File a complaint or something?"

Reuben took a sip of his Coke. She was glad that he at least appeared to consider her question. He swirled his straw around in his cup, staring at the ice shavings and the carbonated bubbles floating to the surface. "We have a saying back home. When two elephants fight, it's the grass that suffers."

Kennedy appreciated the proverb but wasn't sure why he would bring it up now. "So are you and I the elephants or the grass?"

Neither of them laughed.

"I love my home." Reuben wiped his mouth with a napkin before attacking his biscuits and gravy. "But we've got some messed up politics. Tribal tensions that go back to colonial times and even earlier. I'm not saying everyone's corrupted by it. We've got our Martin Luther Kings and our Gandhis. But it's not like in America. Here, you go to a protest or a march, and you assume that makes you some hero. You wave the banner, and then you go home without worrying about your house getting burned down or your family getting death threats. But that's not how I grew up. That policeman we met last night would fit right into Nairobi, especially during election times. I look at people here in America, and I just see a bunch of the world's most privileged kids wasting time and chanting in their picket lines." He finished off his cup of Coke before starting on his second one. "Maybe it's harder for you, being an American. Maybe it's harder for you to admit the corruption. But for me, that's just a fact of life."

Kennedy didn't know what to say. This wasn't the conversation she expected to have. Was this what Reuben had told Dominic last night? Was that why Dominic had pressured her so strongly to keep her complaints to herself, for Reuben's sake if nothing else? It still didn't explain what the elephants had to do with anything. Was Reuben saying that regular folks like the two of them were the grass, helpless to stand up against raging elephants? That instead of wasting their energy trying to stop a fight, they should just get themselves out of the way in the name of personal safety or comfort?

"So you want to pretend like last night never happened?" Kennedy stared as Reuben bit into a greasy sausage patty, and her appetite waned just as quickly as it had perked up a few minutes earlier.

"Yes, last night happened. It was wrong." Reuben let out a little chuckle and wiped his mouth with his napkin. "In fact, there was one point that I thought I might actually wet my pants."

It really wasn't all that funny, but Kennedy found herself smiling. This was the Reuben she knew. This was the Reuben she had grown so close to this year.

He smothered his hash browns in ketchup. "Last night's probably going to be something we remember for the rest of our lives. But things happen, and then you move on."

Kennedy eyed his bowl of Froot Loops and tried to surreptitiously gauge his reaction. "Did you know they're staging a protest today? My roommate's on her way over now."

Reuben smiled. His eyes were soft. "Yeah, that sounds like something she'd do."

Another shared laugh.

"So what now?" Kennedy's insides quivered as she asked the question. "We just hope no one identifies us from that tape?"

Reuben slurped the rest of his second cup of Coke. "I guess so."

"And what if they do?"

He wiped his mouth with his napkin. "Let's just pray they don't."

CHAPTER 12

Kennedy's phone rang as soon as Reuben got up to get himself more food.

"Hello?"

Without any sort of greeting, her dad demanded, "Please tell me you don't have anything to do with that protest they're planning this afternoon in front of the court house."

Hi, Dad. It's good to talk to you, too. "No, I've got class soon, and I'm headed over to the Lindgrens' for dinner tonight."

She could perfectly envision her father's frown all the way from Yanji.

"Well, I don't want you anywhere near it. These things always start out as peaceful demonstrations, but you never know what can happen after that. It's like piling up all your old gas cans right outside a match factory and then acting surprised when you get an explosion."

"I wasn't planning to go. I already said I'm too busy." She had been longing for her dad's advice last night, but now his paranoid protection annoyed her more than anything else.

"So, did you think any more about what you're going to do? Are you going to file a complaint?"

Had she made up her mind on anything? Or had everyone else just made the decision for her? At least if she let it go, she'd be returning to some semblance of normalcy. A little while longer, and all this would be a distant and distasteful memory.

"I think I'll just forget about it and move on."

"That's good." Her dad had this irritating habit of smacking his lips when he agreed with something she said, a quirk she'd almost expect from a toothless old grandfather. "I just got off the phone with my college buddy Jefferson. He's a lawyer now. Got a practice in Worchester. He'd already heard about your encounter when I called."

Kennedy tried not to sigh so loud her dad would hear it on the other line.

"I told Jefferson what you said happened. He believes your story, but honestly, sugar, he said you're lucky the department hasn't charged you both with assaulting an officer. They could have identified you pretty easily by now if they'd wanted to bring you in. The fact that you're still on campus making plans to go to class and visit Carl and Sandy's tonight is proof enough that the department knows their guy messed up. But unless you get evidence, a recording of the confrontation or another witness who watched the whole thing, there's no way your word alone would hold up. It sounds like your best bet is to lay low, let this whole thing blow over, and avoid jumping on any officers' backs in the future."

She knew her father was trying to lighten the situation. Knew that he had probably spent hours out of his day talking with his lawyer friend and researching Massachusetts law. But none of this was funny. None of this would ever be funny. Part of her was so ready to forget last night ever happened, ready to go back to being a regular first-year pre-med student. Ready to talk with Reuben about literature and science and foreign countries, not abusive cops.

But another side of her hated the helplessness she'd experienced when she got pulled over on Arlington. The helplessness she still felt as she listened to every single person she talked to, all the way from an apparently sympathetic policeman to her own father, telling her it was useless to seek retribution. No, not even useless. It was dangerous. If she made a complaint, they'd turn around and lock her up for assaulting a cop. No questions asked. No real justice.

Her dad sighed. "I'm sorry, sugar. I know it's not the answer you wanted to hear. And I told Jefferson, and I told your mother too because she's worrying herself straight off her diet over the whole situation — I told them that if you wanted to seek legal redress, I'd support you. Jefferson's a good lawyer, and he agreed to give us a fair rate. So if you really know what you're getting into and still feel like the right thing to do is bring this officer to justice, we're willing to help you try. We just don't want you to get your hopes up too high, because without any other evidence, well ..." He let his voice trail off. Kennedy was thankful. She'd heard enough threats in the past twelve hours.

"You don't need to let us know what you're going to do right now," her dad went on. "It's probably something you want to think through, and honestly, it might be best to wait until some of the media frenzy dies down. And who knows? Maybe there were other witnesses who will come forward. We can always pray that someone who saw the whole thing will have the guts to stand up and tell people what really happened."

Kennedy watched Reuben walking back toward their table with his second breakfast tray as her dad added, "By the way, how is your friend doing? How's Reuben?"

"He's better now. Couple stitches in his head, and he's walking like he's pretty sore, but the doctors didn't seem too concerned."

"Well, I'm sorry this happened to him. I'm sure he's a great guy, and I know he didn't do anything to deserve to be treated like this."

"Thanks, Daddy." Kennedy felt her throat constricting and wished she had a cup of tea.

"You tell Reuben to get better. Tell him your mom and I are praying for him, and you take care of yourself too, baby girl, ok? I don't want to be seeing your face on Channel 2's webpage for at least another month."

They shared an awkward sort of laugh. Kennedy knew her dad's heart must be just as heavy as hers. After the usual rounds of *I love you* and *I miss you*, they hung up just as Reuben sat back down with his extra tray of food. "You talking to your dad?"

"Yeah, how did you know?

"You just get a certain look on your face. That's all."

Kennedy helped herself to a piece of pineapple from Reuben's fruit salad and glanced at the time. Twenty minutes before they had to be at their lit class. She'd only been awake for a little over an hour and already had the feeling this would be one of those days that would never end.

"What did your dad say?" Reuben asked. "About last night, I mean. Did you tell him?"

"Yeah, but I didn't need to. He's more of a Channel 2 news junkie than anyone on the whole East Coast."

"What did he think about it?" Reuben was studying a piece of cantaloupe as if it might contain all the calculus formulas he'd need for next week's quiz.

Kennedy found herself lowering her voice. Why did it feel as if she were part of some big conspiracy? "He talked to a lawyer friend of his. Says unless someone else comes forward with more concrete evidence, there's really nothing we can do."

"So he wants you to drop the case?" There was a hint of hopefulness in Reuben's voice that Kennedy knew he was trying to hide.

She nodded, and watched a small flicker of relief light up in his eyes. She tested her words carefully, like she might do with a piece of litmus paper she didn't want to get too wet. "Hey, can I ask you something?"

Reuben's body tensed, his fork froze halfway to his mouth.

Kennedy hoped she wouldn't regret her question. Oh, well. Too late to backtrack now. "Is there any particular reason ..." She struggled to find the right words. "About last night. Is there something you've been keeping from me?"

Reuben set his fork by his plate. "Like what?"

Kennedy forced a smile she was sure looked totally unconvincing. "I don't know. Any reason you're scared of the cops finding out who we are?"

He grabbed two grapes and plopped them into his mouth with a shrug. "I've just learned that when the elephants start fighting, it's best to stay as far away as possible."

CHAPTER 13

After a semester and half living in Cambridge, Kennedy thought she should be used to Sandy's hugs by now, but it still caught her off guard when her pastor's wife flung her arms around her as if they hadn't seen each other in years. Once she finally let go, Sandy tossed her long French braid over her shoulder, grabbed Kennedy's hands, and pulled her into their home. "I'm so glad you made it tonight, sweetie. I've been worrying my head off about you since last night." She lowered her voice. "That kind of stuff used to happen to Carl and me pretty regular," she whispered, "back when we were courting in the South. It's a shame to think that people haven't gotten over their differences by now. Heaven knows we've had enough time to change."

Kennedy kept her eyes down and tried not to stiffen when Sandy gave her another hug, this one from the side. "Now maybe you don't want to talk about it, and I don't blame you one bit. If you don't mind, I could sure use an extra set of hands with these pork chops."

Kennedy followed Sandy into the kitchen where the sound of sizzling onions and the smell of homemade bread rolls welcomed her. She washed her hands, grateful for a chance to make herself useful. Anything for some sort of distraction. The afternoon had dragged on just like she expected. She didn't know what it was about the spring that made it even harder to sit in a classroom while the sun streamed in from outside, warming everything up like a giant greenhouse.

"It smells delicious." She wasn't sure what it was about Carl and Sandy's home, but she always felt so peaceful here, as if there was some magnetic field at their front door that stripped away all her stress and anxiety as soon as she entered.

Sandy was bustling over the stove and put Kennedy to work chopping up veggies for a green salad.

"Where's Carl?" Kennedy asked. "Is he still at church?"

Sandy slurped a taste of gravy from a steaming saucepan. "No, he was invited to sit on a panel down at Channel 2. Different community leaders are giving their opinions about the ..." She let out an exaggerated sneeze. "Excuse me. I must have dumped too much pepper in here. Tell me, would you mind tasting this and letting me know what you think? My nose has been a little stuffy all week, and I'm afraid I've over-spiced everything."

Kennedy gingerly sipped from the spoon Sandy held out. "Tastes fine to me."

"Oh, good. Thanks. It must be allergy season or something. Can't smell a thing." Sandy started telling Kennedy a story about her grandson Tyson, who was expecting a brand new sister at the end of May. "You should see the way he loves that baby already. Pulls up his mother's shirt and gives her belly rubs. Says he's playing with his little sister."

Kennedy forced herself to laugh along. She wondered what it would be like to be pregnant, always carrying around a little person you'd never even met. Did it feel like an intrusion, or was it more like snuggling with someone you loved? Did pregnant women always think about their growing uterus, or did they get used to it and go on with life as normal? Motherhood seemed so far away in Kennedy's future. Three and a half more years at Harvard, four years of medical school, then residency ... By the time she was settled enough to even think of having kids, would she be too old? Funny how she never pondered these things except for when she was at the Lindgrens'. What was it about this house that made her long for family? For home?

Sandy prattled on, but Kennedy's thoughts still wandered, her ears ringing with the sound of her own screams as she had tried to protect Reuben. The more she thought about it, the angrier she grew. Maybe she should have gone to that protest after all. After her dad's warning, she had checked the news several times. The only coverage Channel 2 offered was a small article at the bottom of their home screen, but the event itself had been perfectly peaceful. Why was it that strangers were protesting Kennedy and Reuben's mistreatment while the two of them hid like Claudia and Jaime in *The Mixed Up Files of Mrs. Basil E. Frankweiler*, crouching beneath art displays in the Met?

Sandy took some bread rolls out of the oven and set them on a hot pad. The warm, yeasty smell set Kennedy's stomach growling. Other than a few bites of Reuben's fruit salad and a bowl of Craisins for a snack after her lit class, she hadn't eaten all day.

Sandy went back to whisking the gravy on the stovetop. "There's some melted butter in the microwave, hon. Could you grab that basting brush and spread it on top of the roles?"

At the beginning of the semester in her lab class, Professor Adell had posted a quote from a Julia Child cookbook about multitasking in the kitchen. Adell said those same skills would come in handy in the lab, and Kennedy had done enough chemistry experiments as well as assisted Sandy in the kitchen enough times to realize her professor was absolutely right. It also helped to have a partner who could anticipate your moves and know intuitively where to jump in to be the most useful. That's why she was so grateful to work with Reuben. After a week or two of clumsily stumbling over each other in the lab last fall, they could now look at the same set of instructions and perform the entire procedure without having to talk through each specific task. They worked so smoothly, so gracefully together.

She was nearly done spreading the melted butter when the doorbell rang.

Sandy glanced up but didn't look surprised. "Could you get that for me, dear? My hands are a big mess."

Kennedy glanced out the kitchen window to see a multicolored VW bus parked in the Lindgrens' driveway. Maybe she wouldn't have Carl and Sandy to herself tonight like she thought. She dusted her hands off on her pants legs and opened the front door. Nick, the youth pastor from Carl's church, stood smiling on the porch.

"Hey, Kennedy. Glad to see you."

She tried to hide her disappointment. She hadn't expected to be sharing her time at the Lindgrens' with anyone else. Forcing a smile, she stepped aside to let him in. No matter how often she saw Nick, she was always slightly startled by his appearance. From his dirty blond dreadlocks and grungy fashion sense, you'd think he stepped off of a West Coast beach. Today, his T-shirt sported the verse from Revelation where Jesus says, "Behold, I am coming soon," along with a picture of Jesus typing *BRB* into a text message.

"Hi, Nick!" Sandy called from the kitchen, and Kennedy wondered why nobody had mentioned the additional dinner guest. For an awkward moment, neither Kennedy nor Nick knew which one was supposed to be the first out of the small entryway. After a clumsy exchange and a few more apologies than necessary, Kennedy led the way back to the kitchen. The sound of sizzling pork was just loud enough to cover the rumbling in her belly.

Sandy wiped her hands on her apron before giving Nick a big hug. She was as tall as he was, but whenever they were together, Kennedy got the sense that Sandy towered over him. "I'm so glad you made it." She pointed at the dining room table. "Why don't you both make yourselves comfortable? We're just waiting on Carl now. He should be here any minute."

Kennedy wondered what Sandy meant by *any minute* and wasn't sure their definitions would match. She sat across from Nick, trying to guess if he felt just as uncomfortable with this forced arrangement. It wasn't the first time the Lindgrens had gone out of their way to make sure Kennedy and Nick spent time together. Carl kept mentioning how nice it would be if Kennedy found the time to volunteer with Nick during his weekly visit to Medford Academy for an afterschool Bible club. It's possible the church was just short of volunteers, or maybe Carl thought if Kennedy plugged into some sort of ministry at St. Margaret's, she'd feel that sense of belonging she'd lacked ever since her first Sunday there. But then sometimes she'd catch Sandy winking at her husband or smiling mischievously and wondered if there was more to it than the Lindgrens wanted her to know.

She didn't dislike Nick, but that wasn't a good enough reason to pursue a relationship. Besides, she was pretty sure he was interested in someone back in Oregon. He kept a picture on his office desk of a blond girl in a cute tankini, sporting a model's figure and a dimpled smile Kennedy envied. She wished she could be back in the kitchen helping Sandy with the salad. She didn't have anything against Nick. She just didn't like the thought of Carl and Sandy arranging a match for her out of sympathy. Granted, she hadn't made as many friends in college as she'd had in high school, but she had her roommate.

And of course she had Reuben.

She stared past Nick's cross earring and wondered what Reuben was doing now. Was he still upset about their encounter with the policeman or had he forgotten the entire ordeal already? That sounded like Reuben. Never one to dwell on the past. Never one to hold a grudge or harbor negative emotions.

Solid, stable Reuben.

Across from her, Nick cleared his throat.

"So, how's school?" His voice grated her ears with its artificial cheer.

She glanced at Sandy, hoping to find some reason to excuse herself to the kitchen. When no opportunity presented itself, she shrugged. "Not too bad. I'm glad midterms are over. The next few weeks shouldn't be too busy."

"Good." Nick's dreadlocks bounced when he nodded, reminding Kennedy of the apostle bobble heads he had plastered to the dashboard of his painted bus.

"What about youth group?" she asked when the silence grew oppressive. "How's that going?"

A forced smile. More head bobbing. "Good. Good. You should come check it out sometime. We always need volunteers."

Kennedy mumbled her usual excuses about her course schedule and school obligations. She liked the idea of getting involved in ministry. If anything, it might help her snap out of whatever spiritual funk she'd found herself in since she got to Cambridge. It wasn't that she'd rebelled or run away from God. She didn't hate him or doubt him. She didn't even have as much trouble with temptations as she feared she would when she first arrived at Harvard. Her roommate drank nearly every night of the week, partied with harder stuff every weekend, and slept with more partners than Kennedy could name, but so far Kennedy hadn't felt pressured to get involved in any of that stuff. Maybe if she had at least been tempted, she'd find herself more drawn to God and the strength he could give her to resist sin. Instead, she was just coasting through her first year of college. She had drive and ambition when it came to her classwork, but when it came to matters of faith, she was the spiritual equivalent of her roommate — laid back and irresponsible. The only difference was Kennedy felt guilty for her apathy. She doubted Willow entertained those same kinds of self-doubts. She always told herself once she got into the hang of school, she'd get more involved at St. Margaret's, but even now, with three whole weeks before her next major test or paper due, she was reluctant to add anything to her schedule. She was at Harvard for her education, right? So why did she feel so empty?

The door to the garage burst open, and Carl bustled into the kitchen with arms outstretched. He pecked Sandy noisily on her cheek. "And how's my favorite wife today?" He lifted a lid off one of the simmering pots. "You scrape up that squirrel from the driveway?"

Sandy slapped him playfully with a hot pad.

"You know I'm joking, dear." Carl wrapped his arm around her shoulder. "Everything smells wonderful. And how are you two doing tonight?"

Nick was already standing up to shake Carl's hand even though Kennedy figured they must have spent most of the day together at church. After that, Carl gave her a bone-crushing hug that reminded her of her preschool days and a grandpa who'd died when she was only five.

After he let her go, Carl patted her on the back. "Staying out of the news, I hope?"

A disapproving look flashed from Sandy to her husband, who cleared his throat. "Well, let's take our seats. Who's hungry?"

CHAPTER 14

Dinner was even more delicious than it had smelled. Kennedy, who had unintentionally fallen into a mostly vegetarian diet since arriving at Harvard, had to admit she'd eat a lot more meat in the student union if it were as juicy and savory as this. She wondered how many servings Reuben would devour if he were here. Maybe she should have invited him over. Carl and Sandy wouldn't mind.

For a while, the only sounds in the dining room were the scrapings of silverware on Sandy's floral-patterned dishes and Carl's loud chewing and smacking noises. It was the quietest meal Kennedy could remember sharing with the Lindgrens. Sandy diligently kept all the plates at least half full. Whenever Kennedy took more than three bites of anything, Sandy would pass more her way or simply plop another helping onto her plate. Kennedy had spent so much of her college days munching on nothing but dry Cheerios and Craisins she'd probably be anemic if it weren't for these occasional meals at the Lindgrens'.

But tonight, something was different. Carl hadn't given a single commentary on current events, hadn't shared a single political opinion. Nick spent most of dinner avoiding eye contact with everyone, and Sandy made several failed attempts to start up a conversation. She asked Nick about a few of the youth group kids whose names Kennedy didn't recognize, questioned him about an upcoming concert with some Christian band Kennedy'd never heard of. Nick's answers were polite but never more than a single sentence.

Carl, who had been a loud and messy eater for as long as Kennedy had known him, finally finished his last pork chop. He dropped the bone onto his plate and wiped his stained hands on one of Sandy's dainty, rose-embroidered napkins.

"So, you had any more problems with the cops?" Carl's eyes were fixed on Kennedy, so he couldn't see Sandy's disapproving scowl.

"No." She shook her head and caught Nick passing her an apologetic look.

Carl frowned. "The nerve of some people. I just can't ..."

"Honey." Sandy's word was laced with meaning. With warning.

He threw his napkin over his plate. "Now sweetheart, I know you wanted to give Kennedy a night off from all her troubles, but those same troubles will just be waiting for her as soon as she leaves. We're all friends here. We all love each other. So let's talk. You doing ok after everything you've been through?"

The breath Kennedy had been holding rushed out of her. Relief flooded her entire vascular system. No more pretending. No more avoiding the real issue. This was why she loved the Lindgrens so much. And why she was almost always a little nervous whenever she stopped by for a visit.

"Well, it's been kind of crazy ..." She wasn't sure where to begin. How much did Carl already know?

"Sweetheart, it's ok." Sandy grabbed Kennedy's hand. With all the time Sandy spent in the kitchen scrubbing and washing, Kennedy never knew how she kept her hands so silky and soft. "We can change the subject if you want."

Across the table, Nick nodded enthusiastically.

Kennedy stared at her half-full plate, wondering if she'd regain any semblance of an appetite. "Well, I guess you guys saw the video." She was afraid to raise her eyes, afraid of what expressions she'd find on her friends' faces.

"I'm surprised the reporters haven't come to you to get your side of the story." It was the most Nick had said at once all evening.

Memories buzzed through Kennedy's mind like a

swarm of Yanji mosquitoes. Dominic, the praying policeman who'd told her to keep quiet unless she wanted to see Reuben hurt. Her dad's lawyer buddy who told her to give up unless she wanted to get arrested for assault. Willow's friend Othello who treated Kennedy like a KKK conspirator when she didn't blast her story to every media outlet on the East Coast. She felt the onset of a headache and squeezed her eyes shut for a moment. "It's a little more complicated than that."

Carl leaned back in his seat, crossed his arms, and stared at Nick. "Let's say she did give her story to the news. What exactly do you expect would be the benefit of that?"

Nick set his elbows on the table. "Justice. Weeding out a racist cop who has no business wearing a uniform. Making the streets safer for hundreds of other young African-American men so they don't have to face the same humiliation."

Flashbacks of Bow Legs' hands on Kennedy's thighs forced the air out of her lungs. She begged her parasympathetic nervous system to function properly and rehearsed the breathing advice she'd gleaned from all those self-help websites.

Carl raised his eyebrows slightly but didn't respond.

"Think about it," Nick went on. "White cop pulls

African-American teenager out of a car. No warrant. No speeding ticket. All this kid's guilty of is driving while black."

"I believe it was Kennedy who was driving." Carl's voice was soft.

Kennedy glanced around the table. Sandy was still holding her hand.

Nick's dreadlocks grew even more animated the faster he talked. "Ok, so she was the driver. It doesn't really matter. What matters is this white officer pulled this black kid out of the car, and then without any reason …"

Carl jerked his head toward Nick but addressed Kennedy. "How much of the story is he getting right so far?"

She glanced at Nick, her cheeks hot beneath everyone's sympathetic stares.

"Go on," Carl prodded. "Tell him how much of what you went through last night was because Reuben is black."

Kennedy inventoried the faces around her, trying to guess what they expected her to say. "Well," she floundered, "at first I thought that might be some of it. He wanted Reuben to get out of the car, but he told me to stay in my seat."

Carl nodded. "So he told your black friend to step out of the vehicle, and Reuben complied. Peacefully?"

"Yeah." Kennedy remembered how calm he had looked. He wasn't surprised. Wasn't angry. Maybe this story did deserve retelling.

"And then what?" Carl prodded.

Beside her, Sandy strained as if she were about to say something, but instead she just patted Kennedy's hand and stayed quiet.

"He put Reuben in handcuffs. Slammed him against the car."

"So he was rough with him?"

"Yeah."

Carl took a sip of water. "And during this whole time, what was Reuben doing? Was he arguing with him? Threatening him?"

"No. He didn't do anything. I was the one who kept asking why we got pulled over." She was trembling now. She hoped the others wouldn't notice, but she doubted that based on the way Sandy gripped her hand a little tighter.

"See?" Nick banged his fist on the table to accentuate his point. "This is clear-cut racial profiling. The officer didn't have any reason to do what he did. Besides, if it was a regular traffic stop, why would he have the passenger step out of the car? Why the handcuffs? It's what's been going on for decades. White policemen with overinflated egos pulling over young black men just to …"

"So at that point, you jumped on the officer's back, I assume?" Carl interrupted.

Kennedy furrowed her brow. "No, that was later. I got out of the car because I was worried about Reuben. I was worried the officer might hurt him."

"That's what I'm saying." Nick turned to Carl. "Honestly, I'm surprised you're not even more riled up than I am."

Carl grinned. If Kennedy suspected he had a sarcastic streak, she might have said he smirked. "Even more riled up? Why? Because I'm black?"

Nick's obvious embarrassment would have been amusing if Kennedy's memories of the entire ordeal weren't lying just behind her optic nerve, pulsing pain to the back of her eyes and radiating discomfort all the way to her temples.

He frowned into his cup of water. "That's not what I'm saying."

"Oh yes it is. That's exactly what you're saying." There was no trace of a grin now on Carl's face. "You're saying that because I'm black, I need to be just as angry as you, preferably even more so, whenever it comes to any kind of perceived racism."

"Perceived?" Nick's complexion, which still carried the hint of a tan left over from his West Coast surfing days, was now more red than anything else. "All I'm saying is that I'm surprised that you as an African-American man who's endured more than his fair share of prejudice can be so calm after a cop pulls over a black kid, leaves him bleeding on the sidewalk, and gets away with it."

Kennedy could hear the strain in Nick's voice, could sense the tension in his body and almost see the pulse of his carotid artery. Carl, on the other hand, still leaned back in his chair, and Kennedy got the sense he could just as easily be discussing Paul's introduction to his epistle to the Galatians as anything else. He turned toward her, his eyes calm. She wondered if he worked deliberately to achieve that degree of peace or if it was just some supernatural gift or a fortunate personality quirk, a blessing from genetics. He smiled at her tenderly. "And how did it feel for you, a white woman, when this big bad white policeman beat up your black friend?"

She had a feeling Carl expected a certain reply out of her but couldn't guess what it was. "I didn't think about it in that way while it was happening." She spoke slowly, partly so she had time to plan her response and partly because she was trying to mask the tremor in her voice. "He said some really rude things to Reuben, racial slurs I mean, but he was just as crass to me."

Her throat tightened. She hadn't realized how much she was shaking until Sandy wrapped a strong arm around her and said, "I think maybe we should save this discussion for another time."

Carl smiled sheepishly. "You're right, sweetie. Of course. Kennedy, I'm sorry. I know how upsetting this must be."

Nick cleared his throat. "I'm sorry, too." For once, his dreadlocks fell perfectly still.

Everyone stared at their plates. Nick scraped a few green beans around in his gravy.

"So." Sandy turned to her husband. "Do you have everything ready for Sunday's sermon?"

He shook his head. His usual jocular smile was gone. "I'll be spending most of tomorrow at the office. Still have a ways to go."

More silence.

Kennedy wanted to apologize. As if Carl and Nick's argument was all her fault. As if she should have known better than get into an altercation with a cop that would spoil a perfectly delicious meal.

"I have a meeting tomorrow with one of the teens." Nick's comment seemed to appear out of a vacuum, an infinitely dense black hole. As soon as he spoke, he shoved a bit of bread roll into his mouth. Nobody responded. From the living room, a clock ticked, reminding Kennedy of her mother's grandfather clock back in Yanji.

"Well." Sandy spoke with exaggerated cheer and clasped her hands together. "Carl and I haven't made it official to the church yet, but we're so close to both of you, I wanted to share some good news." She glanced at her husband, who nodded approvingly. She reached for an envelope from the countertop and pulled out a photograph. "We just got word that we were matched for adoption. We're hoping to bring our little boy home from South Korea this summer."

Kennedy reached for the photograph that Sandy proudly showed off. Studied the smiling boy. He appeared so emaciated it was hard to guess his age, maybe eight or ten years old. He had two skinned knees, a dimple in one cheek, and a smile that showed two missing teeth in opposite sides of his mouth. Kennedy didn't know what to say. Were you supposed to congratulate the adoptive parents or was that just for pregnancy announcements?

"He's adorable."

Sandy was beaming. It was a special expression she only wore when she was talking about her children or grandchildren.

Nick reached for the photo and raised his eyebrows. "I didn't know you guys were planning on adopting overseas."

"Neither did we." Sandy chuckled. "There was one point before we started fostering that we thought about it, but we ran into problems."

"Yeah." Carl's booming voice was a striking contrast to Sandy's maternal prattle. "Back in the day when prejudice really was a problem in our country, adoption agencies wouldn't consider interracial couples. They said we ..."

"So," Sandy interrupted, her voice still chipper and cheerful as ever even as she glared at her husband, "we don't know much about him yet. We know his name's Woong, and we know he's had a pretty hard life so far. The orphanage can't tell us his real age. I've just been praying so hard about this adoption, and I knew as soon as I saw his picture he was ours. I can't explain it, really. I took out that photo, saw those little missing teeth, that grin — he looks pretty mischievous, don't he? Well, soon as I saw him, I knew in my heart that God had called me to be his mother." She laughed. "I feel like Sarah. Look at me. Already a grandmother with two more grandbabies on the way, and God's decided to add one more son to our family." Her eyes glistened. "It's just so hard to wait now that I've seen his face."

"That's great." Kennedy wondered what it would be like to love someone you'd never met. What if this Woong boy was even naughtier than his picture hinted? What if he had learning disabilities or medical issues nobody knew about yet? What if he didn't want to leave the orphanage? What if he hated his adoptive parents and gave them nothing but grief for his entire childhood? The Lingrens had agreed to take him in without knowing any of those things. Not only take him in, but love him as their own son. Well, if anyone could do it, Carl and Sandy could.

"How long ago did you start planning another adoption?" she asked.

Sandy let out another giggle. Kennedy was amazed at how she looked ten or fifteen years younger just talking about her newest child. "We've been thinking about it for some time now, but we didn't want to get our hopes up. Like Carl said, we had our troubles with international adoptions in the past."

Nick rolled his eyes. "Yeah, back in the old days when racism still existed."

Kennedy bit her lip, hoping Carl wouldn't be baited into another round of verbal boxing.

Naive of her.

"I'm not saying racism doesn't still exist. I'm just saying it's not the number one problem facing America today like Gordon Clarence and his followers want everyone to believe."

"You surprise me sometimes." Nick frowned. "I would

think that someone who's been through what you have — like being told 'back in the old days' you couldn't adopt a child from another country because you were black and your wife was white — I wouldn't think you'd forget everything you've gone through so quickly."

Carl ignored Sandy's pleading eyes. "Nobody's forgotten, son. Nobody except these revisionist historians who make their fortunes keeping racism alive. Tell me, what would happen to Gordon Clarence and his million-dollar book deals if racism weren't an issue anymore?"

"But you ..." Nick tried to interject, but Carl cut him off.

"Yes, you're absolutely right. I've experienced racism firsthand. My whole family did, for generations back. From the plantations to Jim Crow to the bus boycott when my mama walked six miles to work both ways for a year. Did you know my father spent the night in jail after sitting in with Dr. King at a whites-only restaurant? You want to talk racism? You want to tell me how bad it was? I don't need that history lesson, son. I lived it. My daddy lived it. My grandparents and their parents and grandparents lived it. So when you jump online, and you read a story by some college-age journalist who hasn't ever seen the inside of a jail cell or the wrong end of a riot baton, when you read his gut-wrenching story about a white idiot committing a crime against his black brother, you and everyone else out there shouts racism. But you know what? There's no one race that holds the monopoly on murder or drug abuse or gang violence or any other vice you name. So when a white cop assaults a black college student with absolutely no provocation, is it possible he's racist? Sure. But is it also possible that he's just a deplorable human being?"

Kennedy glanced around the table. Nick frowned, occasionally picking at a green bean, and Sandy set down her picture of the South Korean orphan and offered it sad glances from time to time. A few beads of sweat had coalesced on Carl's forehead.

"You asked why I'm not more upset about this police incident. The truth is, I'm livid. Kennedy knows I'd do anything for her. I'll walk her down to the police department and help her file a complaint right now if that's what she wants. But I don't think that's what you're really asking. I think you're asking why I'm not aligning myself with the so-called *Reverend* Clarence and waving picket signs and strong-arming the police department into firing their racist cop. Because I don't have all the information yet. He might be racist, sure. Or maybe he's a bad cop who hates everyone equally. I don't see the feminists out there protesting, do you? I don't see them picketing and riling up the masses because a male cop pulled over a female college student. In fact, what disgusts me the most about this entire ordeal is that everybody seems to forget the fact that there were two victims of this crime. You're so ready to call this a case of white-on-black police brutality. Then where does that leave Kennedy? Are you going to tell her that her skin's not dark enough so she didn't actually suffer? Who's rallying for her, I'd like to know? Who's waving signs and demanding justice on her behalf?"

Kennedy felt the flush creep up her face when everyone fixed their eyes on her. Sandy held her in a protective half hug.

Nick fidgeted with one of his dreadlocks. "I can see what you're saying, and I certainly didn't mean to imply that what Kennedy went through wasn't bad. But then there are other cases that are even more clear-cut, cases where white cops harass black teens who aren't doing anything other than driving or walking down the street in the wrong color skin. What about that? Don't you think there needs to be some kind of oversight? Some sort of accountability?"

Carl crossed his arms. "Tell me something. If you're a cop and I told you to track down a dangerous suspect, five-foot-eight, close-shaved haircut, no facial hair, and that suspect happens to be black, is it possible that you might mistakenly pull over one or two innocent citizens for questioning?"

"Yeah. And that's the whole problem with racial profiling."

"So you're suggesting that instead of telling you to be on the lookout for a close shaved, five-foot-eight black man, I should just tell you to be on the lookout for a five-foot-eight man? Wouldn't that become gender discrimination? Should I just say a five-foot-eight person? Would that solve the problem of profiling?"

"I'm not saying that. What I'm saying is a lot of black men are scared of the police. They're scared of walking down the street and getting stopped by cops and searched and harassed."

"And why are they harassed?" Carl asked. "Is it because ninety-nine percent of cops are out to get blacks? Is that what it is? An occupied war zone, as Mister Reverend Clarence likes to call it? Or is it possible that these black men are harassed because they're conditioned from birth to despise the police, to disrespect the police, to take every instance of a white cop talking to a black man as a clear case of oppression? Are there bad cops? Sure. Are there racist cops? Absolutely. Should those problems be dealt with? Yes. But are Clarence's protests going to make the streets safer for our black brothers and sisters? No. And I'll tell you why.

"Let's say Gordon Clarence has his way. Let's say he turns Reuben into a martyr for the black civil liberties movement. Let's say a more comprehensive video comes out showing that Officer What's-His-Name was clearly out of line. Everybody's going to call it prejudice, a case of white oppression. So the police force makes all their officers go through cultural sensitivity training. Tells them they can't pull someone over based on their skin color. Reminds them they could get sued or lose their jobs if they show any sort of prejudice. What happens the next time two white cops are chasing down a black drug dealer or a black rapist? What happens when everyone's hunting for a black suspect who's accused of murdering his girlfriend? What white cop with half a mind is going to pull a black man over because he matches the suspect's profile? What white cop who values his job is going to use that Taser on a black criminal who's resisting arrest? All the sensitivity training's going to do is teach cops — the majority of whom I'm going to say are decent, moral human beings — it's going to teach them that their hands are tied when it comes to dealing with black suspects or black criminals. Now, how is that going to make our streets safer?"

Carl paused for breath, and Sandy took advantage of that moment to scoot her chair back noisily. "Well, it looks like everyone's finished with dinner. Who's ready for some dessert?"

CHAPTER 15

They made it through Sandy's pineapple upside-down cake without any more arguing. Sandy told them about the progression of their adoption journey, starting from the time last summer when the Lord had put it on their hearts to open their home to one more child. She was always boisterous, but tonight, she was even more animated than normal as she spoke about little Woong.

"The hardest part now is waiting. I don't remember praying for patience, but I guess that's what God must be giving us."

Kennedy couldn't understand everything adoptive parents go through, but she got the part about patience. For so long, her life had felt like one big waiting room. Waiting for high school to end so she could leave Yanji and return to the States. Then, once college started, it was waiting for midterms or finals to be over so she could finally rest. Waiting to see her parents again after a whole year at school. Waiting to return to Yanji for the summer, even though she'd been in such a hurry to leave last fall.

There was more to it, though. More difficult experiences that tried her patience. Waiting for reprieve from her anxiety. Waiting for whatever improvements those stupid counseling sessions were supposed to bring. And Reuben. First waiting for her mind to catch up with her heart so she could admit she had real feelings for him. Feelings beyond a simple crush. And then waiting to find out if he felt the same way.

Would she ever know?

She glanced surreptitiously at the Lindgrens' clock.

"I'm sorry," Sandy apologized. "It's getting late. I shouldn't have kept you so long. It's the adoption. Gets me babbling."

"It's ok." Kennedy forced a smile even though thinking about Reuben turned her overstuffed stomach slightly sour. What was he doing now? How long would it take before things could go back to the way they were before?

Carl pushed his seat back from the table. "I'll give you a lift back to campus."

"You don't have to do that," Kennedy replied. "It's not dark out yet. I can just take the bus and catch the T."

"You'll do no such thing, young lady." Carl turned his pockets inside out. "Now where did I put my keys?"

Nick scooped up his dirty dishes. "Actually, I need to hit

the road, too. Some of the youth group boys and me planned a late-night X-Box tournament at my place." He reached over for Kennedy's dirty plate. "I'll drop you off at your dorm. No problem."

Sandy smiled and joined Nick clearing off the table. "So I guess that settles it. Thank you both for coming over and sharing our good news with us. I'm sorry if I talked your ears off."

"Don't believe a word she says," Carl quipped. "At least not the part about her being sorry. If I had known this would happen once we decided to adopt again, I might have asked her to wait another ten years until I had hearing aids I could turn down on command." He leaned over and pecked Sandy's cheek. "Thanks for dinner, babe. It was delicious."

Kennedy and Nick both expressed similar sentiments. Once they got the table cleared and endured a drawn-out goodbye on the porch, they finally made their way to Nick's VW bus parked in the Lindgrens' driveway.

"Is that a new paint job?" Kennedy asked, pointing to a cross made out of colorful handprints on the side door.

Nick let himself in. "Yeah, I guess you could call this an ongoing project. Every few months, one of the youth group kids comes up with an embellishment. I try to be as accommodating as I can. Gives the teens a sense of ownership in the ministry, I guess. Although you might have heard how Carl had to veto the picture of John the Baptist's head on a platter."

Kennedy chuckled and fastened her seatbelt. "Thanks for the ride. You sure it's not too much out of your way?" She didn't even know where Nick lived.

"I don't mind. Gives us an excuse to be together. I mean, without Pastor Carl and Sandy breathing down our backs. You ever get the feeling they're trying to play chaperone?"

Kennedy forced a laugh, even though she felt her face heating up like a beaker on top of a Bunsen burner. "I'm sure they mean well."

"Yeah." Another chuckle, just as forced as hers. "They certainly do."

The pause that followed reminded Kennedy of those moments in class waiting for the teacher to hand you back a test you were afraid you'd failed.

"What are you listening to?" she finally asked when she couldn't think of anything else to say.

"Oh, that? It's my uncle and some of his buddies. They've got this folk, grunge, worship band mix going on in Oregon. Call themselves the Babylon Eunuchs. You know, because Shadrach, Meshach, and Abednego were probably ... Well, never mind. Do you like it?"

He turned the volume up, which made the slightly off-key singing even more discordant. "It's not bad," Kennedy lied. At least it gave her an excuse to not have to hold a conversation. Unfortunately, as soon as the first song ended, Nick turned off the CD. "You know, now that we're alone, I've been wanting to ask you something."

Kennedy felt her body tense and fought her muscles to relax. Her mind raced back to all her previous encounters with Nick, including a pseudo-date over Christmas break when they went out together for clam chowder.

"What is it?" She held her breath.

"Do you think it's wise for Pastor Carl to be so political?"

Kennedy blinked, more confused than relieved. "What?"

The Peter, James, and John bobble heads nodded sagely while he spoke. "Like tonight, for example. It just seems to me like the leader of a racially diverse megachurch in Cambridge would understand how polarizing some of his views can be."

Kennedy had to admit she didn't know as much about American politics as either Carl or Nick. She could only guess what he was hinting at. "So you're upset about the racism thing?"

Nick shrugged. "Partly. But not just that. Don't get me wrong, he's a great pastor, and I couldn't hope for a better boss. He's a good friend too, which is why I don't want to call him out on it. But the American church is on its deathbed, at least when it comes to conservative evangelical Christianity. These folks like Carl, they're not taken seriously anymore. People don't come to church to hear arguments against gay marriage or abortion. They want to see grace. Where's the grace in berating women for something they did to their child years or decades in the past?"

Kennedy frowned. "So does that mean you're for or against abortion?"

"Against. Naturally. But really, is abortion the issue, or is poverty the issue? Did you know that eighty percent of women who get abortions do it because they don't feel like they can afford to raise another child? So what should we do, should we focus on banning abortions, or should we spend that same energy and resources on lifting women out of poverty so they don't seek out the procedure in the first place? Do I like abortion? No. But are we really doing any good when all we talk about is which pro-life candidates to elect?"

Kennedy frowned. She wasn't following Nick's reasoning, and she had the feeling that she was too uninformed to ever catch up with his logic.

"Around the country," he went on, "Christians are seen as judgmental hypocrites doing what they can to strong-arm the government into agreeing with everything they preach. I mean, I'm all for the Bible, but seriously, does it really matter if a courtroom hangs up a copy of the Ten Commandments or not? When Jesus tells us to feed the hungry and free the oppressed, was he really talking about whether or not school kids say *under God* in the pledge of the allegiance?"

Sensing he was waiting for a response, Kennedy muttered that she hadn't thought through those issues lately. And by lately, she meant at all, but she didn't mention that part.

"So then there's Pastor Carl, and I already said he's one of my favorite men in the world. He's totally out of touch with the times, but people keep coming to his church. St. Margaret keeps growing, and I don't know why."

For once, Kennedy felt like she could contribute intelligently to the conversation. "It's probably because people see how much he and Sandy love others. Isn't that what church is supposed to be about?"

"You're probably right." Nick turned his uncle's dissonant blend of banjo, guitar, and inept vocals back on and glanced at her long enough to crack a grin. "You're a smart girl. I guess that's why they let you into Harvard."

The second half of the drive back to school wasn't nearly

as awkward as it started out. Nick dropped her off as close to her dorm as he could without needing to park, and Kennedy smiled to herself when she pictured what the other students would think of the pimped out Christian bus. As she made her way to her dorm, she realized she was more relaxed than she'd been in weeks. When she got to her floor and heard Willow and some guy talking, she wasn't even that upset. It was a Friday night, after all. If Willow really wanted the room to herself, Kennedy could text Reuben to see if he wanted to meet her at the library to go over some calculus.

She pushed the door open, but her smile faded when she saw Dominic in his uniform standing by Willow's desk.

"Oh, there you are." He didn't smile.

Neither did her roommate.

Willow took in a noisy breath. "I was just talking with Officer …" Her voice trailed off.

Dominic shuffled his feet. "I'm afraid I have some bad news."

Kennedy's abdomen felt as if it were crashing to the ground like a poorly executed inertia experiment.

Dominic glanced once at Willow and then cleared his throat. "I'm here about your friend, Reuben. He's just been arrested."

CHAPTER 16

Kennedy's lungs seized up like the bulb on the tip of a Pasteur pipette. She didn't know who to look at. It felt as if both Dominic and Willow had betrayed her.

Her roommate frowned sympathetically. "You want some tea?"

Tea? At a time like this?

Arrested. Had she heard that right? Was it possible they were wrong? She turned to Dominic. "Were you the one who brought him in?" Her tone dripped with anger and accusation, but she didn't care.

He shook his head. "No. This is all out of my hands here. I just wanted to let you know. It'll be on the news soon, and I didn't like the thought of you finding out that way."

"Why?" Kennedy demanded. "You said the department wouldn't bother us. You said they'd be scared of the real story coming out."

Dominic offered the slightest hint of a shrug. "That's what a lot of us are wondering, too. Best guess is the chief was getting too much pressure. The media wasn't buying the whole 'I forgot to call for backup' story. And then came Gordon Clarence and his followers with their protests, turning this whole thing into some kind of a witch hunt. The chief had to do something. Take some kind of action to save face."

Kennedy couldn't believe she'd let this man pray with her. She couldn't believe another Christian could stand by and tell her these things while still wearing his police uniform. Why had he stopped by at all? Was he just here to gloat? Here to warn Kennedy not to get involved? Or …

"What about me?" She wanted to sound forceful, but her voice betrayed her fears.

Dominic offered a small smile, which looked out of place on his sheepish face. "You're fine. The chief looked into your background and apparently decided you weren't worth messing with."

"Because I'm white?" All Carl's platitudes about racism being a sin of the past now sounded as nonsensical as the Dodo's ramblings in *Alice in Wonderland*.

Dominic's expression grew stern. "No. Because of your background. The chief knows a good lawyer will rip his guy to shreds if this case goes to court. He doesn't want to touch you with a ten-foot pole."

His words took time to settle, like droplets of oil slowly

coalescing in an aqueous mixture. "So it's because my parents can afford a good attorney?" she finally asked.

Dominic didn't answer her question. "I'm really sorry. I came by to tell you if there's anything I can do ..."

"Yeah, there is," Willow interrupted. Kennedy had forgotten for the moment her roommate was listening in to their conversation. "You can get her friend out of jail."

"I wish I could." Dominic sighed. "Unfortunately, my hands are completely tied."

Willow scrunched up her violet-tipped hair. "Yeah, that's not good enough." She pointed her finger toward his chest. "You know what's even more dangerous than a corrupt cop? A halfway decent cop who sits in his patrol car full of self-righteousness and smugness and says he wishes he could do something about the bad ones but he can't."

Kennedy wasn't sure if she should try defending Dominic or not.

"It makes me sick to think of how many of you there must be," Willow went on, "going home to your nice little nuclear families, shaking your heads because one of your colleagues just acted like history's biggest jerk, feeling smug because you're one of the good ones and at least you're 'doing everything you can.' You make me nauseous."

Part of Kennedy was ashamed her roommate was

subjecting Dominic to this verbal bashing, and part of her was glad Willow had the courage to express what she couldn't yet articulate.

Dominic adjusted his uniform. "I better go."

"Yeah, you better," Willow spat.

He looked at Kennedy. "Is there anything else I can do for you?"

She wanted to ignore him, throw him out of the room with Willow's insults echoing in his ears, but instead she asked, "What's going to happen to Reuben?"

Dominic frowned again. Kennedy realized he could be handsome if it weren't for the strained, worried look in his eyes.

"It's hard to say. He's from Kenya, so they're going to get the embassy involved. Nobody wants this to escalate further than it needs to. They'll have an arraignment, probably charge him with assaulting an officer. If he's convicted, my guess is they'll move for deporting him. By then everyone will have forgotten about the whole incident, so the chief won't have any reason to make him serve more time."

"Do you think they have enough evidence to convict him?" Kennedy asked.

Dominic shrugged. "Depends on what kind of jury he gets."

Kennedy tried to cling to some sense of hope. "But you said if another witness came forward ..."

A sad, heavy sigh. "It's been all over the news. If any more witnesses are out there, we would have heard from them by now."

"But it's possible?" Kennedy wasn't sure if she was making a statement or asking him a question.

"It's possible." He met her eyes. "But I wouldn't bank on it."

What about prayer? she wanted to ask him. Didn't he believe in prayer anymore? Maybe if they all start asking God for a new witness to materialize ...

"He's got school. We haven't finished our lab report. He can't miss that."

"I think right now, your friend has more urgent matters to worry about than his classwork."

"So there's nothing we can do?" It wasn't right. It wasn't fair. This was America, where everyone was promised an equal chance, where justice was supposed to be a non-negotiable guarantee.

Dominic stepped toward the door. "We can pray. And hope another witness comes forward with the full story."

CHAPTER 17

As soon as Dominic left, Kennedy plopped into her roommate's beanbag chair with a groan.

Willow filled up an *Alaska Chicks Rock* mug. "Have some tea." She passed it to Kennedy. "Man, I thought he'd never go. He's got a lot of nerve just showing up like that."

"How long was he here before I came?"

Willow sat down at her desk and kicked her feet up on the bed. "Not long. At first, I thought he might be coming to arrest you. Othello said something like this would probably happen, you know."

"He did?"

Willow nodded and poured herself some tea. "Yeah. I guess he's been following this police brutality stuff for quite a while now. Says that once they get pressured, the department does what it can to vilify the victims. It's one thing for a cop to shoot an unarmed black kid. But if the kid has a criminal record, or if drug tests show he was high when he was murdered, most people go back to their day-to-day lives and assume he must have deserved it."

"This is a little different than a shooting, don't you think?" Kennedy took a sip of Willow's bitter medicinal tea.

"Not really. The only difference was Reuben wasn't killed. You're lucky that way. It could have been a lot worse."

Kennedy couldn't believe she was just sitting here sipping tea while Reuben was probably paralyzed with fear in some jail cell. What would happen to him there? Kennedy didn't even know what happened to American citizens who got arrested. What about an international student? Would they extradite him? Her mind was spinning like a pulsar star. Would she even see him again?

Willow let out a dramatic sigh. "Listen, I'm really sorry you're going through this. It sucks no matter how you look at it." She stood up and grabbed her hand-painted fashion scarf.

"Where are you going?" Kennedy didn't want to admit how much she hated the thought of being left alone.

"I'm gonna go talk to Othello. He'll want to know about this. Maybe he'll find a way to help Reuben."

"The only way to help Reuben is if another witness comes forward." She hated the resignation she recognized in her own voice. Was it really that hopeless?

Willow passed her an almost empty container of raw honey. "Here, take as much as you want with your tea. I can always get more."

Kennedy accepted the Mason jar, trying to find a way to ask Willow to stay with her without having to beg. For the first time, she wondered where she put her therapist's business card with his after-hours phone number. She couldn't just stay here like this. For a minute, she considered tagging along with Willow but remembered how uncomfortable she felt during the arguments around the Lindgrens' dinner table. She couldn't bring herself to get up from the oversized beanbag chair.

"You all right?" Willow put in her long, feathered earrings and stared at Kennedy's reflection in her small desk mirror.

Kennedy lowered her face into the steaming mug. "I'll be fine." She hoped it wasn't a lie.

Once Willow left, Kennedy dissolved two big spoonfuls of honey into the herbal concoction and thought about Reuben. It wasn't fair. She almost wished Dominic had come and arrested her, too. Then at least she'd know her dad would do everything in his power to free her. If Kennedy was arrested, her dad would hire the best defense lawyers in the greater Boston area. The officer that assaulted them would be lucky if he could ever show his face in Massachusetts again. Who did Reuben have to advocate for him? Who would speak up for him?

She glanced at the time. It was already morning in Yanji. She grabbed her phone, grateful to see it still had plenty of charge. She was breathing faster than normal as the call connected. Would he be there?

"Hello?"

"Daddy?" Her voice squeaked. She swallowed down a little more tea. She couldn't cry. Tears wouldn't solve anything. They were just as useless and nearly as paralyzing as her anxiety. She had to get through this conversation. For Reuben.

"What is it, princess? What's the matter?"

She had hoped the news would have already made it onto Channel 2's website, which her dad kept up with more religiously than any locals Kennedy knew. She bit her lip, trying to form the words, afraid of the way they would confront her with their hideous reality once she gave them voice.

"They arrested Reuben."

If she had been talking with her mom, she would have been blubbering by now, but with her dad it was different. He didn't waste time asking about how Kennedy felt or worrying about her emotions. He bypassed all those fluffy preliminaries and jumped right into his formal, businesslike interview. "What did they charge him with?"

"I don't know. Something about assaulting an officer, I think." She took another scalding sip of tea, thankful to find her vocal chords weren't too strained.

"Where are they holding him?"

"I'm not sure."

"Have you talked to anyone else? Do you have any reason to believe you'll be arrested next?"

"No. There was a policeman here just a minute ago. He's the one who told me about Reuben." She wanted to tell her dad more, but he was firing questions at her as fast as a proton slinging its way through a particle accelerator.

"Have you talked to anyone from the press?"

"No."

"Good girl. You keep it that way, all right? I'm on Channel 2's page. They've got the story right here. Looks like they still haven't mentioned your name. That's good. By the sound of it, if they wanted you too, they would have gotten you by now. I don't think you need to worry, princess."

Couldn't he understand? How calloused did he think she was? "I'm not worried about me." Her larynx tightened.

She took a gulp of tea and focused on the feel of the honey sliding down her throat. "I need to know how to help Reuben."

For the first time since he picked up the phone, her dad was quiet. She could picture his scowl as he stared at his computer screen.

"He's an international student, right?" he finally asked.

"Yeah."

"Well, there's gonna be red tape. Bureaucracy. The good news is that means it will give him and his lawyer time to …"

"He doesn't have a lawyer." Kennedy wanted to scream. For being such a business genius, her dad could be completely daft at times.

"He doesn't have a lawyer," Kennedy repeated with a little more restraint.

"Then the courts will assign him one …" Her dad's voice trailed off. Kennedy hoped he was finally grasping the seriousness of Reuben's situation. She pictured him in his Yanji office, his desk strewn with paperwork, his urgent-message file cluttered to overflowing. He probably had a dozen pressing matters that needed his immediate attention, and she was asking him to ignore all that and help her find a way to get Reuben out of jail. Should she tell him everything? Should she tell him about the drowning, suffocating weight in her chest when she imagined him getting deported back to Kenya? All thoughts of romance aside, how could she make it through the rest of her semester without him? Reuben was the only good thing that had happened to her this entire school year. Everything else had been an anxiety-riddled headache at best, traumatizing torture at worst. Through it all, through kidnappings and murder attempts, through lab reports and research papers, Reuben had encouraged her. Supported her. How could she step foot into the chem lab Monday knowing that she had abandoned him?

She knew her dad. Knew he was probably getting ready to lecture her on the American justice system, how if you were patient enough, the truth would rise its way to the top like the most soluble substances on a paper chromatogram. After what she had seen, after talking to Dominic who had first-hand experience with the police force, she wouldn't believe a single word of it.

How could she make her dad understand? How could she tell him how important this was to her? She felt like a petulant toddler, ready to stomp her foot and throw a fit until she got her way. But what else could she do to save Reuben? How else could she help him? Dominic had mentioned prayer, but what good was that when the entire justice system was willing to sacrifice an innocent student to protect the reputation of a corrupt cop? Back in Yanji, when the Chinese police came into her parents' home to question them about their business, their visa paperwork, or any hint of missionary activities, Kennedy had hidden upstairs in her room wishing to be back home in the States, imagining life in a country where the police were there to protect you, not harass you. Had she really been that naïve? Had she really been that foolish?

She heard her dad let out his breath. "Give me a few minutes, sugar. I'll call Jefferson and see if there's anything he can do."

Kennedy bit her lip, wondering if she should say what she was thinking. Would it make things worse, or would it be better for her dad to know the complete truth at the beginning? She took a choppy breath. "I don't think his family has a lot of extra money for lawyers and things."

Another sigh. Heavier this time and slightly more dejected. "He won't have to worry about that, princess. Just hold on, and I'll call you back in a few minutes."

The small stream of relief that washed over Kennedy reminded her of a bright ray of sunshine in the middle of winter — enough to give you hope without warming you up at all. Still, it was a start. "Thanks, Daddy."

"You're welcome." If they had been face-to-face, he would probably make some sort of joke about how Kennedy was responsible for his growing bald spot or his rapidly diminishing bank account. But there were no jokes this time, just the small clicking sound of her dad hanging up his office phone. Kennedy stared at her screen after the call ended. Her dad would try to help. There was nothing to do now but wait.

For the next several minutes, all Kennedy could think about was a video series for prospective medical students her dad had made her watch when she decided to apply to Harvard's pre-med program. In one of the lectures, a doctor who survived cancer talked about medical testing from the patient's perspective, how hard it is to wait for results that could spell life or death for yourself or your family member. His words hadn't impacted Kennedy much at the time — she had been more interested in the immunologist's speech on AIDS and other disorders that impacted the immune system — but it was all she could think about now while she waited for her dad to get hold of Jefferson. She tried not to think of how hard it would be to contact a lawyer at 8:30 on a Friday night. What if he didn't return her dad's call until Monday? What would that mean for Reuben? She didn't know anything about jails or prisons. She didn't know if they had visiting hours or any way for the inmates to interact with the public. Part of her worried that if she went to the jail to check on Reuben, someone there would recognize her from the infamous piggyback attack video and book her for the night as well.

Well, if that's what it'd take to get the attention of her dad's lawyer friend …

She should probably be doing her own research, too. Wasn't that what the internet was for? But she knew if she turned on her computer, she'd never get past all the news articles of Reuben's arrest. It was too heinous to have a hundred different reminders bombard her from a hundred different websites. She remembered the way Othello had explained it. If the police wanted to keep their own reputation untarnished, it made sense they'd try to ruin Reuben's. What would they say about him? Did he have his cell phone with him? Could she text him to see how he was doing?

All we can do is pray. Dominic's words rang through her mind like the taunts of a playground bully. *All we can do is pray.* Wasn't that the spiritual equivalent of a doctor telling her dying patient there was nothing left to do but discuss palliative care and make hospice arrangements?

All we can do is pray. Was that the Christian way of saying there was no hope whatsoever?

She bowed her head over Willow's half empty mug. Even the sight of the tea leaves reminded her of Bow Legs, how he had made such a big deal of that stupid Ziploc bag in the glove compartment. She stared at her phone. If it had just taken the video like she'd told it to, none of this would be happening. Bow Legs would be the one behind bars, and she and Reuben would be at the library studying calculus or at the student union finishing up their lab report.

Why had God allowed her phone to fail her? Had he stopped paying attention for those few seconds? Was he too busy helping believers on the other side of the world? But it didn't work like that, did it? Kennedy knew there were people suffering more than she was, but still, did that mean God thought her problems weren't significant enough to waste his energy on? Had he simply forgotten to intervene?

She thought about Carl and Sandy, about all the injustices they suffered in the past. How did they remain so loving and hopeful? What was the secret and the source of their joy? What did Kennedy have to do to discover that same sense of peace she always felt with them?

Her heart leapt like an electron jumping up an energy level when her phone rang. Her dad. Was it a bad sign that he was calling back so soon? He couldn't have gotten a hold of the lawyer, explained everything to him, and come up with a plan to save Reuben in five minutes, could he?

"Hi, Daddy."

"I just got off the phone with Jefferson." No greeting, no *Hi, princess.* What did that mean? Was her dad calling with bad news? Had the lawyer already looked into the case and agreed that the only thing left to do was pray?

Thankfully, her dad didn't waste words. "He said the same thing as yesterday. Without more evidence or some key witness coming forward, there's not much to do. I know it's too late for it now, but if you ever find yourself in that sort of situation again, it'd be a good idea to turn on your phone's video camera and ..."

Kennedy fought the urge to throw her cell across the room. "I did take a video." She wasn't trying to yell, but she couldn't help it. "I started recording at the very beginning when he handcuffed Reuben. It's the stupid phone. There wasn't enough memory ..."

She choked back tears of frustration. Why had she ever left Yanji? Why had she ever gone to Harvard? She could have gotten her college degree online without ever having to leave her parents'. What had she been thinking?

"Calm down, sweetie." It was just like her dad to say something like that. He didn't even bother telling her to pray. He knew how hopeless the situation was. So that was it.

Reuben would spend a few weeks or months in jail, go to trial, and get deported back to Kenya in disgrace. Never complete his studies. Never tell Kennedy the secret he'd planned on sharing Thursday night. In a way, this was all her fault. Why had she suggested they go see *Aida*? Why couldn't they have just spent the evening in the library like normal?

"I'm sorry about the phone, princess. I'll do some research. Maybe there's someone in your area who can retrieve the memory for you. You say that you got the entire confrontation recorded?"

"Everything. It was in my pocket, so you can't see it all, but you can hear what was going on."

"And you think the recording would be enough to prove Reuben's innocent?" There was a hint of doubt in her father's voice.

"Of course he's innocent. I already explained to you, that officer …"

"I remember what you told me last night," her dad interrupted. "I'm just saying that sometimes people remember certain events in different ways …"

Kennedy had heard enough. "I told you already, he didn't do anything wrong. Neither of us did." She was starting to understand why Dominic had warned her to drop the entire case in the first place. If the media could skew events until her own dad doubted her, how could she expect the general public to take her side?

"All right," he conceded. "If you think the video will help, I'll see if there's somewhere you can take your phone to try to get the memory retrieved. It's probably a long shot, but without more evidence, Jefferson says there's not much of a case."

"So he's just going to let Reuben get deported?" She couldn't believe this was happening. She couldn't believe the country that boasted such liberty and freedom could arrest someone as kind and considerate as Reuben to keep a corrupt officer out of trouble.

"I didn't say that." She sensed the tension in her dad's voice and remembered why she had been so eager as a high-school student to leave home. "All I said was he didn't think there was much of a case. I hired him to look into it for us anyway, and if you have evidence on your phone that might make a difference, we need to pursue it."

Kennedy was ashamed of her outburst. She injected what she hoped was enough humility into her voice and said, "Thanks, Daddy."

"Don't thank me yet. I'm no Atticus Finch."

Kennedy smiled at her dad's reference to one of her

favorite novels. "I'm really glad you're at least trying."

"Well, I know a certain young lady who can be pretty persuasive when she wants to be. And I figure it must be a special boy to have caught her heart like that."

Kennedy felt the warmth radiating up to her cheeks. "It's not like that, you know."

"Well, whatever it is, I'm glad I'm able to help. Let me jump online and see what I can find about your phone. I'll call or text you when I have more information."

Kennedy was used to sudden waves of homesickness crashing over her without warning. She choked down a large sip of tea and thanked her dad one more time.

"Yeah well, I just hope this Reuben fellow understands how lucky he is that you care so much about him."

CHAPTER 18

Kennedy's head was throbbing by the time her dad sent her a link with information on retrieving lost photos. The procedure required a certain app, so while she waited for it to download, she got herself ready for bed. It wasn't even nine yet, but her mind was heavy with exhaustion. Sandy's fatty pork chop sat in her gut like a chunk of cement. It was the most meat she'd eaten since Christmas Eve at the Lindgrens'. Things had felt so normal back then. Reuben came with her, and they had spent the evening laughing over every single mistake they'd made in the chemistry lab during their first semester of school.

Life had been so simple. Tests and homework and lab write-ups. Kennedy could handle that. What she couldn't handle was the horrid uncertainty, the fear of Reuben's fate, the sense that God must have abandoned her or else he wouldn't have thrown her into the midst of such a convoluted mess.

Was God angry about her feelings toward Reuben?

She'd heard Carl say from the pulpit that the Lord was a jealous God. Did that mean he was mad not to be in the center of Kennedy's attention, so he was going to punish the person she cared about most? Was God really that possessive? Would he really act so petty?

After the app downloaded, she followed the directions to retrieve her lost photos. She wasn't sure what good it would do. The video she needed wasn't lost. It hadn't recorded at all. Still, there was always the small shred of hope. Maybe God was looking out for her after all. Maybe this would be his way to prove it.

As soon as the program finished loading, Kennedy scrolled through the recovered files. Most of them were pictures of lab results she hadn't needed in her write-ups. There were also two photos she and Reuben had taken at the *Nutcracker* ballet when they went last Christmas. The images were blurry, which was probably why she'd deleted them, but she stared for several minutes at the smiles on her and Reuben's faces. Had she ever felt that happy before she met him?

She told the app to save the photos back into her regular gallery. She wasn't ready to get rid of them yet. They might be the last pictures she'd ever have with him. She wished she could have talked to her dad's attorney friend. She needed to know what would happen to Reuben. Would he be deported if they found him guilty, or would they keep him in prison here? She wasn't sure which option was worse. What would his family think? What would his parents say?

As expected, the recovered photos didn't include anything from her traffic stop. She should have known it was foolish to hope. Should have known God wouldn't come through for her. What did he care? He was probably too concerned with the world's missionaries and pastors to fret much over a nineteen-year-old college freshman and her best friend.

She blinked her dry eyes. There had been a time when her faith had come so easily. Mom and Dad loved Jesus, so she did too. Mom and Dad said he died on a cross and came back to life, so who was she to argue? She didn't doubt any of it even now, but what did it matter whether or not Jesus was alive if he just let injustice run rampant? Was the hope of a distant future spent in the heavenly clouds supposed to compensate for a lifetime of sorrow here on earth?

And what about those people who were even more oppressed, the child laborers and sex slaves suffering throughout the globe? Did God see them? Did he care? And if he did care, why wouldn't he do something to free them?

It didn't make sense, and Kennedy was too tired to try to

figure it out. This line of reasoning would just make her more depressed anyway. She may as well go to bed. Maybe things would look brighter in the morning.

She doubted it.

She let out a small groan as she laid her head down on her pillow. She hadn't realized how tight her muscles were. Willow had been trying to talk her into joining some co-ed yoga group all semester. Said it'd be great for Kennedy's anxiety, but she was too busy. Besides, why would she want to wear spandex and sweat on a germ-infested mat alongside two dozen other strangers?

She glanced at her phone one more time as if the missing recording might magically appear on the photo retrieval app. No such luck.

Of course.

Her phone buzzed in her hand, startling her. She didn't recognize the number, but whoever it was could wait. She didn't want to talk to anybody, not unless it was …

Her hand shook when she answered the call. "Hello?"

"Kennedy? Is that you?"

In an instant, her pituitary gland flooded her entire brain with endorphins. Relief collided with nervous excitement. Joy coursed through every single vein in her body. "Reuben?"

"It's me."

"Where are you? Are you ok? Did you get hurt?" She couldn't decide which question she wanted answered first.

"I'm ok." She heard the strain in his voice, recognized his attempt to stay positive. "They said I could make a phone call, and I didn't … I wasn't … Well, I called you."

"I'm so glad. I've been worrying all night about you. What are they saying? What's going to happen now?"

"I have some court appearance on Monday. That's about all I know so far."

She tried to imagine what her dad would say in a similar situation. What advice would he give? What would he tell Reuben to do? "You don't have to answer any questions, you know. You should demand to have a lawyer present if they need to talk to you." Wait, was that right? Or was it different for international students? Did he have the same rights as everyone else, or would it work some other way?

"It's ok. I've already talked with someone from the embassy. It looks like if I plead guilty, I'll most likely just get deported. They probably won't give me an actual jail sentence."

He was talking like a crazy man. "You can't do that. You were acting in self-defense. We both were. You have to let the guy know that …"

"I already made up my mind. I'm showing up in court Monday, I'm pleading guilty, and I'm hoping they'll just send me home instead of making me serve time here."

He wasn't thinking clearly. He was scared. Confused. Who wouldn't be at a time like this? "Listen, my dad's already hired a guy for you. A really good lawyer he knows. He thinks you have a good chance." She hoped he wouldn't hear the doubt in her own voice.

"That's nice of you to say, but I don't want you worrying about me."

She squeezed her eyes shut. "You can't just give up. What about your studies? What about all you've worked so hard for?"

Betrayal. That's what it felt like. Betrayal. Did Reuben seriously believe he'd be better off taking the blame for Bow Legs' crimes? He had worked too hard his first year at Harvard. He and Kennedy both had worked too hard. What about those countless hours studying together? What about their friendship?

She plugged in her phone, determined to keep it from losing charge. "Listen, I'm going to try to figure out how three-way calling works. I want you to talk to my dad. He knows a lot about these things. He'll tell you himself ..."

"It's not that simple." Reuben's voice was so quiet,

Kennedy could hardly make out the words. She bit her lip and forced herself to listen. When inmates get to make one phone call, what does that mean? One phone call a week? A year? Total? Would this be the last time they'd ever talk to each other?

"Listen, the thing I was going to tell you last night, I ..."

No, it couldn't happen like this. He was acting as if he'd never see her again. He was scared. She couldn't let him say something they would both regret later.

"Don't worry about that right now." She wished her dad were here. He would know what to do. He would have the right words to say. She had to give Reuben some kind of hope. "Listen, I think there's a way my dad knows to get a recording of the attack off my phone." The more she talked, the more she forced herself to believe it was true. Any other alternative was too horrific to fathom. "Once we get that video, everyone's going to see you're innocent. The court, the police department, everyone. So don't do anything right now. Wait until my dad's friend gets in touch with you. He'll know what to do."

"You shouldn't be so worried about me." Where was this fatalistic attitude coming from? Did he want Kennedy to be the first to say the thing they'd both skirted around?

She clenched her jaw and resolved to be like her dad.

Unemotional. Detached. Reuben didn't need tears or sentimentality. Not right now. He needed the kind of friend who would knock on every judge's door and pester every single member of the police force until he was free.

"Listen, we've been through a lot together." Now she was the one who sounded like she was saying goodbye. Was she? And if so, would she live the rest of her life in regret if she didn't tell him everything? Her heart was racing in her chest, pulses of fear paralyzing her vocal chords. She took a deep breath. She could do this. She remembered her dad. Meticulous. Professional.

"Just hang on until Monday. By then, I'm sure your lawyer will have come up with your defense. It's going to be ok. Don't think about jail sentences or going back home or any of that. Just think of this as a short break from school. You'll show up to court Monday, the judge will see there's absolutely no case against you, and the only thing you have to worry about is whether or not I do a good job on our lab report to get us both a good grade. Ok?"

There was so much more she wanted to say. Like how scared she was at the thought that she might be wrong. She might not get that video. She probably wouldn't. And even though the lawyer had agreed to represent Reuben, he was far from optimistic. But none of that information would help

Reuben right now. All he needed to know was Kennedy was advocating for him. Because she couldn't stand the thought of a single day in class without him. Because she had already allowed her mind to wonder what might happen if the two of them both found the courage to admit how much they meant to each other. Because they shared something deeper than friendship.

Those were the things she wanted him to know, but she couldn't find the words to tell him. Not like this. Not with him stuck in some jail.

"Let's just make it to Monday," she said as much to herself as to him. "Things are going to work out. I promise."

CHAPTER 19

As soon as Kennedy ended her call with Reuben, before she even got the chance to let her tears fall freely, the door flew open. She glanced up at Willow and for a second felt the embarrassment her roommate must have experienced a dozen times whenever Kennedy walked in on her making out with one of her boyfriends.

"Everything ok?" Willow asked, slipping on a few dangly bracelets and grabbing her bohemian cardigan.

Kennedy forbade her voice from betraying her. "Yeah. I just got off the phone with Reuben."

"Really? Did he say anything? Are they treating him ok? I hear cops can be kind of jerks in cases like his."

It wasn't what Kennedy wanted to hear. "Yeah, he sounded all right." Was that true? She knew Reuben so well, but how could she begin to assume what he was feeling, what he was experiencing right now?

"Well, I'm not staying long." Willow threw her lip balm and a few organic throat lozenges into her braided handbag. "I just came back to grab a few things before Othello and I take off." She stood and took Kennedy by the arm. "And by a few things, I'm talking mostly about you." She raised Kennedy to her feet. "Come on. There's a protest outside the courthouse. You should see how many people are already there to support your little Kenyan buddy." She frowned when Kennedy hesitated. "Don't worry. It's gonna be peaceful. There's gonna be some ecumenical prayer time even, leaders from different faiths. Come on. You do believe in prayer, don't you?"

It'd be heretical to deny it. She glanced at her clock. She probably couldn't fall asleep yet. At least this way she wouldn't feel like she was sitting around doing nothing. But still, that kind of crowd ...

Willow draped an arm around her shoulder. "Come on. I think this will be good for you. If it gets to be too much, I'll drive you home. Deal?"

Whenever Kennedy thought about the people who'd helped her most in Cambridge, Reuben and the Lindgrens always came to mind. She realized now she had overlooked someone else just as important. Her roommate.

"Ok. Thanks."

Kennedy grabbed her coat. Attending a peaceful protest wasn't talking to a lawyer or researching immigration laws online, but it was better than doing nothing.

CHAPTER 20

The closest parking spot Willow could find was four blocks away, so she, Kennedy, and Othello got out of the car and started to walk. Kennedy was glad for her new trench coat, a cute birthday present from her dad last February. A spring chill had settled in the air as soon as the sun set. She could hear the crowds several streets away. She strained her ears, searching for any hint of anger or potential violence. Her abs were already quivering. Another reason she was thankful for her coat.

Willow sided up next to her. "Still doing ok?"

Kennedy nodded even though she already regretted letting Willow talk her into coming here. How big of a crowd was there going to be, and how many of them would be sick and contagious? How long would Willow and Othello want to stay? What did anyone hope this mass undulation of human bodies would accomplish?

The crowd spilled off the sidewalks and onto the side streets. At first, Kennedy thought someone must have brought in searchlights, but then she realized the glow was coming from the hundreds of lit candles the people were holding as they stood in front of the courthouse steps. Someone was praying into a loudspeaker system. There was something familiar about his cadence even though Kennedy couldn't place the voice. "Father God, gracious Savior, we come before you as a humbled people. We come before you as a society that is broken, that is riddled with injustice and oppression. We come before you as individuals who are sick, sinful, enslaved to all kinds of depravity. We confess that we don't deserve your mercy. We confess that we don't deserve your kindness towards us. But you are a God who delights in his people. You are a God who delights to extend forgiveness. So forgive us, Father. Forgive us our trespasses, our prejudices, our bigotry, our chauvinism, our selfish ambitions. Forgive us our hatred, merciful Lord. Show us once again had to love one another. Heal our society."

Kennedy frowned. The crowd of candleholders was far too thick for her to hope to see the speaker. She didn't just know his voice. She recognized the way her soul burned while he prayed. Where had she heard prayer like that before?

Dominic?

She was so upset over everything Reuben was going

through, she had almost forgotten how Dominic prayed with her that first night they met. He was an enigma. How could a Christian with such passion for God serve in the same police force that had imprisoned her friend? Was he just here to assuage his guilty conscience?

The prayer continued, and the crowd grew quieter with each refrain. "Calm our spirits, Lord. Where there is fear, grant us your peace. Where there is anger, grant us your mercy. Where there is hurt, grant us your healing. Heal our relationships. Heal our justice system. Heal our broken families. Heal our society. We have no hope other than you, Father."

At first, Kennedy found it strange that he hadn't even mentioned Reuben. But on the other hand, he had addressed more in those few minutes than she could have ever hoped to cover if she'd spent an hour in prayer by herself. It was the difference between a nurse wrapping up a gushing wound and a surgeon going in and cauterizing the source of the bleed. Dominic was a powerful man of prayer, but that still didn't explain what he was doing on the speakers' platform. There were far too many people for this to be an open mic night at the prayer vigil. Was he here as a member of the police force? What would his superiors think?

"Thank you very much, Reverend," announced an

unknown voice. "That was Pastor Dominic, Protestant chaplain for the Boston Police Department."

Chaplain?

The noise increased exponentially. Whatever sense of peace had rested on the crowd during Dominic's prayer, it was gone now. There was no shouting or anything Kennedy might have expected from a protest like this, only the rustlings from several hundred fidgeting people. Coughs and murmurs threatened to drown out the soft-spoken Episcopalian minister who was the next to offer up her prayer.

"Come on." Willow tugged on the belt of Kennedy's trench coat. "Othello went up ahead. Said he saw some of his friends up there."

Before Kennedy could respond, Willow began her complicated weave through the crowd of candleholders. Kennedy wondered what the fire chief would say at the sight. She pictured the sidewalks covered in candle drippings tomorrow morning. Is that all that would come from this prayer vigil — dried wax and litter? Was any of this doing any good at all?

All we can do is pray. Sure, this was better than the rioting and looting that had accompanied other accounts of police hostility across the nation, but would it help Reuben in the end? If God wanted Reuben saved, shouldn't he have done it already? And what about all the people praying who weren't even Christian? This was an ecumenical event. What if a Muslim went up front and lifted up a prayer to Allah, or a Universalist prayed to some great cosmic being that sounded more like the Force in *Star Wars* than the God of the Bible? What would the Lord think of all this? Was he offended to have his name plastered alongside so many other religious deities, or was he just happy that people came out to pray at all?

It was only a few seconds into the Episcopalian's prayer that Kennedy lost sight of Willow. Oh, well. She'd catch up with her and Othello later. It wasn't worth coming into bodily contact with a hundred different strangers carrying who knew how many billions of germ cells just to keep up with her roommate. She was surprised Willow had come to a prayer vigil at all. Willow claimed to be agnostic, and she usually took every chance she could get to blast the evils of organized religion, convinced as she was that the vast majority of the world's problems throughout history could be blamed on Christians.

For the most part, Kennedy and Willow had gotten along so well because they avoided arguments. Sometimes Kennedy wondered if God wanted her to be more confrontational, if he was upset with her for letting her roommate speak so badly about the church, but she hadn't studied well enough to come up with counters to Willow's unyielding stance. Besides, her dad had always taught her you couldn't argue someone into the kingdom of heaven. Was Kennedy doing the right thing by keeping the peace, or was that just a fancy way of saying she was too ashamed of the gospel to stand up for it? She really didn't know.

She stretched her spine and strained her neck for one last chance to catch a glimpse of Willow. At least they both had cell phones. They could always connect with each other later. Kennedy wasn't very comfortable around Othello and was glad for a chance to avoid his crowd anyway. As the quiet woman up front finished her prayer, Kennedy froze. What if Othello told his friends about her? What if he told them that she was the mystery woman from the video? So far, Kennedy had avoided all that media attention and drama. She knew Willow would respect her privacy, but what about her friend?

She should have never come tonight. Every single person here knew about the piggyback attack. Most of them had probably seen her face in the video. She didn't have the most unique features in the world, but what if someone recognized her? The candlelight was as bright as a hundred streetlamps.

How had she let Willow talk her into coming? And why had she allowed herself to get separated from her roommate?

A tap on her shoulder. Kennedy whipped her head around. This was it. The end of her privacy. Her false sense of security.

"Excuse me, Miss." A middle-aged man was frowning at her. "Do you have the time?"

Kennedy let out her breath, wondering if it was possible to get drunk on relief. She reached into her pocket. Where was her phone? "I'm sorry ..." She tried her coat as well as her jeans. Had she really been that stupid? Had she left it in her dorm? "I can't seem to find my cell," she muttered only to find that the man had moved on and was asking someone else.

No phone. How would she get a hold of Willow when it was time to go? She hadn't even paid attention to where they parked.

Why had she ever come here?

"... And Lord, we come humbly to ask that you would bless our brother Reuben. Give him peace. Let him rest well tonight in comfort and safety. May you free his heart from all fear." Kennedy wished she could shut her ears. While Dominic had prayed earlier, she found it odd he didn't mention Reuben once. But this was even worse, this woman who had never met him, asking God to grant him a good night's sleep in his jail cell. This stranger didn't know anything about Reuben, didn't know how many sisters he had, how he doted on his nephews and nieces back home, how steady he could keep his hands when it came time to do a titration procedure in the lab. Kennedy bit her lip. When had it gotten so cold? She needed her heavy winter jacket, not her trendy fashion coat. She clenched her jaw to keep her teeth from chattering. Why would anybody ever want to be in a place so crowded?

"And Lord, we also pray for the young lady involved. Wherever she is, we pray for her protection tonight."

Tightening in her lungs. The hint of a diaphragm spasm.

"We pray that you would bless her."

One gasping breath that did nothing to draw in air. A second attempt, and then a third before the oxygen wheezed in.

"We pray that you would keep her in your perfect peace."

Her heart racing. Her brain's limbic system in complete chaos.

"We pray that you would keep her safe."

She had to get out. So many people. So many bodies. A middle-aged woman coughed right next to her. Was it influenza? Tuberculosis? Who would willingly expose themselves to so many people's contagions?

"Thank you for the love you show us."

Get away. There was no other option. She'd go find Willow's car and wait for her there. But what if she got lost? What if she ran into a cop? Were the police out looking for her? Dominic had said she wasn't in any danger of getting arrested, but hadn't he said the same thing about Reuben just last night? Besides, Dominic was nothing more than the chaplain. What would he know?

The chaplain? Why hadn't he told her that sooner?

"Thank you for your mercy and grace."

Kennedy's heart was about to burst its way out of her pericardial sac. There was no way her body could maintain this level of adrenaline. Could a nineteen-year-old have a heart attack? Would anyone notice her dying in this sea of strange faces?

Another gasping breath. Wheezing. Begging for life. For safety. For refuge.

She couldn't support her weight. Her blood CO_2 must have skyrocketed. Soon, acidosis would ravage her body systems. There was no way she could expect her muscles to work properly. She just had to get away from the crowd, otherwise she'd fall and just as likely get trampled as die from heart failure.

Choking on something that was half a sob and half a cry for help. There were hundreds of people here. Couldn't one of them see she was about to pass out? Her head felt as if it would float off her shoulders. She would collapse any second. Her only hope was that her body would wait until she was on the fringe of this mass of humans before it gave out on her completely.

"Are you ok?"

She didn't stop to address the young mother carrying a baby in a front sling. She couldn't slow down. She had to get out.

"Can I help you?"

She became vaguely aware of multiple pairs of staring eyes. She was so focused on getting away from the people, so intent on forcing air into her lungs that she hadn't realized she was crying, if that's what you could call the sobbing, gasping, wheezing noises that came out of her mouth. She stumbled blindly ahead.

"Hey, can I help you?" When did people grow so nice? When did society ever care so much for one individual? And if Boston was really filled with such conscientious citizens, why was Reuben spending the night in jail?

Someone grabbed her arm. Someone she didn't know. She wasn't strong enough to shake him off. "Leave me alone." Her voice was so garbled she hardly understood the words herself.

There it was. She recognized the bank across the street. Willow's car was somewhere over there. The crowd had thinned out, too. She had made it.

Almost.

With the faint sound of the minister's *amen* dying in her ears, Kennedy tripped and barely managed to throw her hands down to the pavement to break her fall. Someone knelt beside her. "Can I do something for you? Is there someone I can call to help you?"

It was hard to focus on his words. She knew you couldn't die from a panic attack — she had looked it up once — but what if this was something else? What if her heart really was giving out because of all the stress she'd been under? Maybe she should have taken those yoga classes with Willow after all. She wasn't ready to die. There were so many plans she had for her life.

Tears streamed down her cheeks. From a distance, someone called her name.

"Kennedy!"

Something in his voice, still so far off, beckoned to her. She could hardly focus on the Good Samaritan who knelt on the sidewalk beside her.

"Kennedy?"

Air rushed back into her lungs. She drank it in like a marooned Ben Gunn dying of thirst. She could almost feel her brain swelling with the welcomed influx of oxygen.

"You know her?" the stranger asked.

"Yeah. Kennedy, can you hear me?"

Relief and humiliation both clashed in her chest. "Pastor Carl?" Her voice broke. A second later, she was sobbing into his shoulder, oblivious to the crowd, the kindly stranger, and the prayer vigil for Reuben that persisted just a block away.

CHAPTER 21

Kennedy could only guess how long she and Carl sat on that cold pavement. He didn't say anything, didn't offer any false reassurances or tell her to calm down. Didn't accuse her of overreacting or offer any pastoral guilt trip that if she only prayed or read her Bible more she wouldn't be such a mess.

Once her sobbing quieted down and she could breathe somewhat normally again, he checked her limbs for any injuries, asked if she had hit her head when she fell. And then he held her longer, as if his only reason for being near the Boston courthouse tonight was to make sure she felt safe.

"I'm glad I saw you," he finally said. "They invited me here to give a prayer, but I was running late. Couldn't find my keys. Must be providence, because otherwise I probably wouldn't have seen you ..." He didn't finish his thought, and Kennedy was thankful to avoid hearing the eye-witness account of her own embarrassing meltdown.

"I don't know what happened," she said. "I was fine one minute, then all of a sudden ..."

"Shh. Don't you worry about it." Carl glanced at his wristwatch. "Listen, I'm already late, and there's no way I'm leaving you here alone." He leveled his gaze to look at her as sternly as he could pull off. "You didn't take the T alone, not this late at night, did you?"

"No, I came with my roommate, but we got separated."

"Well, let me call my friend and tell him I can't make it. He's the one who arranged all this. I'm sure he'll understand." Carl held his old-fashioned flip-phone to his ear.

"I don't want you to miss out." Kennedy took in a deep breath to prove to both herself and Carl that she could. "I don't mind ..."

"Stuff and nonsense," he interrupted and then held up his finger. "Hello, Dominic? Can you hear me?"

Kennedy still couldn't understand why he always needed to shout when he talked to someone on his cell.

"Yeah, it's Carl. Something came up, and I'm not gonna make it." He yelled for a minute longer about how sorry he was for missing the vigil and then ended the call.

"That's a good man," he said as he put his phone in his back pocket. "Most godly saint this police force has ever seen."

"Was that the chaplain?"

"That's right, Dominic. You know him?"

"A little. We met at the ... He was at the hospital last

night. He didn't tell me he was the chaplain. I just thought he was an officer."

Carl let out a little laugh. "That's Dominic for you. Most humble, unassuming man I know." He groaned as he stood up and then reached down to help Kennedy to her feet. "You up for a little walk? I had to park behind the bank."

She nodded. "I'm better now." Part of her wanted to leave Carl and go find Willow, pretend none of this had ever happened. But then she saw the ocean of bodies and heard the sound of an acoustic guitar strumming over the loudspeaker. She would never make it back in that crowd. "You sure you don't want to stay? I could wait here while you go pray."

Carl jerked his head toward the courthouse, where some folk singers with only slightly more talent than the Babylon Eunuchs were singing an over-embellished version of *Imagine*. "I'm not that big of a Beatles fan these days, truth be told." He grinned and extended his arm. "Want a little extra support?"

Kennedy was pretty sure she could walk on her own, but she took Carl's elbow and allowed him to lead her slowly down the street until the sounds of the crowd and mediocre singing faded into the darkness.

CHAPTER 22

Carl insisted that Kennedy spend the night with him and Sandy in their Medford home. She didn't have a way to let Willow know where she was, but Carl volunteered to drive all the way to her dorm to get her cell phone while she and Sandy had tea. Of course, by tea he meant cookies, cinnamon rolls, and any number of Sandy's baked goods, but Kennedy wouldn't turn that down. Not tonight.

Sandy was pulling a tray of banana nut muffins out of the oven when Carl dropped her off at his house. Sandy set the muffin tin on the stovetop and wrapped Kennedy up in a 360-degree hug. "Carl told me you'd be coming. I'm so sorry about Reuben."

It had only been a few hours since Kennedy was here eating pork chops, but the first whiff of cinnamon and vanilla set her stomach grumbling.

"You had such a hard night, sweetheart." Sandy led Kennedy into the dining room and sat her down at the table. "You just get comfortable. I have tea heating up right now, and you can keep me company from there while I finish up my baking." She glanced at the door that led to her garage. "Where's Carl?"

Kennedy explained how he went to get her phone so she could call Willow and let her know she wouldn't need a ride home.

"And how is your roommate, sweetie? Are you two still getting along well?"

Kennedy accepted a cup of tea and added a spoonful of honey. "Yeah. I'm kind of surprised by it all, but we're getting along great. We're going to room together again next year.

"That's fabulous, darling. It's so nice when God brings friends like that into our lives."

"I don't know that God had much to do with it in this case. I mean, Willow is about as far from Christianity as you can be."

Sandy threw some cream cheese into an old-fashioned electric mixing machine. "Sometimes those are the ones who fall for God the hardest when their time comes."

Kennedy allowed herself to chuckle at the thought of Willow turning her life around that drastically. Sandy whipped up some frosting in her mixer, and Kennedy wondered what life would be like if she hadn't known the

Lindgrens, if she arrived at Harvard without any kind of support system, like Willow who flew here all the way from Alaska. How did people endure the loneliness? The Lindgrens' home wasn't just a place to satisfy her sweet tooth or keep her from becoming anemic. It was a place where Kennedy found love, unconditional acceptance, a sense of peace she'd never been able to fully experience in the dorms.

More than anything, this was home.

Sandy pulled a tray of fresh-cut fruit from her fridge and set it on the table. "I thought we'd start with this while the muffins cool." She winked. "That way, we can at least pretend that we're eating healthy."

Kennedy took a pineapple chunk and remembered her conversation with Reuben in the student union. He had wanted more than anything to avoid a confrontation with the police. Why? Was it because he didn't want to get arrested? Did he have some sort of premonition about what would happen to him? Or was there more to it? She replayed her conversation with him on the phone. What was it he'd wanted to tell her?

Sandy took a dainty bite from an oversized strawberry. "So tell me, darling, how are you doing with all this?"

Kennedy had no idea what Carl said to her when he'd

texted Sandy from his car. Did she know about the panic attack? The last thing she wanted to do was to relive those few awful minutes at the vigil, recall how scared she'd been, certain her heart would give out from adrenaline overdose, certain she would die quite literally from fright.

How was she doing? How was she supposed to know? How could she take the time to assess her emotional well-being right now while Reuben was locked away in some cell? Would he be alone or with others? Was he safe? The first day of the semester, her children's lit class had discussed a book depicting a gang rape while the main character was wrongfully imprisoned. At the time, she wondered how the story could have found its way through any juvenile fiction press's editorial process.

Sandy patted her hand. "It's all right if you don't know how to answer. Sometimes our brains know it's time to switch to survival mode, get us through the crisis. We don't always get a chance to deal with the emotional side of things until later on."

It made sense, but in another way, wasn't Kennedy here at the Lindgrens' home because of an overdose of unruly emotions? If there was something she could take to deaden her senses just a little, she could handle it all. She was used to stress. She was used to pushing herself out of her comfort zone. What she wasn't used to, what she would never get used to, were these debilitating panic attacks that could swell up in her, overwhelm her at the slightest provocation and the most inopportune times. Her anxiety had already cost her so much. Sleep. Energy. Her grades would start to suffer if she didn't get things under control soon. She could only guess what all this trauma was doing to her health, but she'd be surprised if she made it through another year at Harvard without her gastrointestinal tract breaking out into a dozen ulcers.

Kennedy stared at the plate of fruit and wondered what they would feed Reuben in jail. She wouldn't blame him if he hated her after this. Wasn't she the one who suggested they go see *Aida* in the first place? Wasn't she the one he was trying to protect before Bow Legs knocked him to the ground? And what had she done to help him? Whined to Daddy like a spoiled brat, but what had that accomplished? Would her dad's lawyer friend even get to Reuben's case before the weekend was over? Even when she tried to get the evidence she'd need to prove Reuben's innocence, she had already filled up her phone's memory with too many stupid pictures from chem lab. Why hadn't she kept better track of her storage space? Why hadn't she deleted all those useless photos once she didn't need them? It wasn't as though she'd ever have to pass pictures of her synthesized salicylic acid on to her descendants.

"What are you thinking about, sweetie?"

At first, Kennedy couldn't splice any words together.

"What's on your mind?"

Sandy's question was as strong as capillary action, slowly defying gravity and drawing a response out of Kennedy's mouth.

"He called me today. Reuben did. He got one phone call, and I couldn't even help him." She shook her head. Tears spilled down her cheeks like tiny drops of rain on oily asphalt. "There's nothing I can do."

Sandy nodded. "That's one of the hardest things to go through when you're unable to help someone you love. I know it's not easy, little lamb, but God gives us the strength we need ..."

"But he hasn't," Kennedy protested. "That's just the thing. I've prayed for strength. I've prayed for patience to get through all these things. I've prayed to be a good example to Willow, but I'm such a mess." She looked down at her torso as if Sandy might see how filthy and defiled she really was. "It doesn't make sense. I've done all the right things. I'm setting aside time each day to read my Bible. I'm praying all the time." She let out a mirthless laugh. "And I'm a bigger nutcase now than I was a year ago."

Sandy didn't speak right away. Didn't chide Kennedy for her blasphemous accusations. Didn't remind her that all things work together for good or offer any of the other platitudes Kennedy was expecting. Instead, she took a long sip of tea and sighed. "I wish I had the answers for you."

So that was it? That was the best Sandy could do — Sandy, who was married to the pastor of one of Cambridge's most prominent churches? Sandy, who volunteered twenty or thirty hours a week at the pregnancy center and ran the children's ministry and babysat her grandson three days a week and still found time to bake cookies for lonely college students? She was saying there was nothing that Kennedy could do, no way to make all the pain and trauma disappear. Then what was Kennedy even doing here? Why was she searching for answers to impossible questions if it was just a big waste of time? She imagined God up in heaven, shaking his head, telling her that her quest was as hopeless as Atticus Finch taking on the Tom Robinson case.

Kennedy stared into her mug. "Yeah, I guess it was pretty silly for me to expect the impossible."

Sandy shook her head. "We never stop expecting the impossible, sweetie, but we have to temper that faith and that hope with the reality that this world is a fallen place.

Sometimes evil prevails, but only for a time and only if it somehow works into God's master plan. Now, I don't pretend to understand how it fits together, or how God uses bad events to bring about good, or why he allows evil to persist when Jesus has already conquered. My soul yearns more every day for heaven when I think about how much God's children are suffering in this world. I think about our son, our little Woong so far away in South Korea. Carl and I are his parents, but we can't hold him. We can't comfort him. We can't snatch him out of whatever horror he's had to live through. We can only wait. Do you know how that tears a mother's heart up? But what can we do? We can claim that God is evil for allowing so much pain and injustice. We can lose all hope and turn our backs on him like Elijah was tempted to do in the wilderness. Or we can stick our heads in a hole, ignore the hurt and the suffering around us because it's too much for our narrow view of God to handle. Or we can accept the fact that this world is full of misery, and we can do what we can — limited though our efforts may be — to be the love of Christ to those who are hurting. To be hope to those who are discouraged. To be family to those who've been abandoned. To be healing for the brokenhearted. Balm for the suffering."

Sandy smiled softly. "That's the third option, my dear. It

means waking up every day and asking God how you can shed his light into the darkness around you. It means opening your heart to the feeble, the downtrodden, the afflicted. It means speaking up for the oppressed, loosening their chains. The real saints, the ones who are taking God's message of love seriously, are the ones who can see the pain around them, feel the impact of sin, and instead of losing heart or giving into despair, they covenant with God that they are going to push back that darkness. Reclaim the lost for Christ. Resist the decay and pollution and oppression that's brought the world to where it is today. That's the power we have in us, precious. It's a big responsibility."

Kennedy had to chuckle.

Sandy laughed back. "What is it, dear?"

"You went from motivational speaker to Spiderman's uncle without stopping for air."

Joy lines crinkled around Sandy's eyes, even though Kennedy wasn't sure she understood the reference.

"You see what I mean, don't you, darling?"

Kennedy nodded. "Yeah. It's just hard."

Sandy refilled her mug. "No, it's just life."

Kennedy reached for some cantaloupe. "I guess what I mean is I worry about what kind of witness I'm being for Christ. I mean, I don't know if Carl told you, but I was a big sobbing mess before he brought me here. So I love what you're saying about bringing hope to the lost and all that, but when I try to be strong I end up falling flat on my face more often than not."

"Who said you have to be strong?" Sandy asked the question so pointedly Kennedy had to run through their entire conversation to see if there was something she had missed.

"I never claimed you were supposed to be strong to accomplish all those things." Sandy brought the muffins over to the table and started to frost them.

"But I can't even make it through a simple prayer meeting without hyperventilating and sobbing in front of complete strangers. How is that supposed to show God's victory?"

Sandy set two muffins on Kennedy's plate. "It's during those times that we're the weakest when God can show himself the most dramatically. And I'm not talking about just taking away your panic attacks, pumpkin, although if he wanted to do that, he certainly could. What I'm talking about is you having the freedom and courage to live out your life — stress, anxiety, and all — in front of others with a vulnerability and grace that can only come from above. Think about your roommate for a minute. What are her biggest reasons for hating Christianity?"

"She says the church is full of judgmental hypocrites."

"So, she thinks that all Christians put on a mask and act phony to cover up their struggles. But you can show her how that's not the case, how God can take someone at her weakest, at her most anxious, at her most traumatized, and how he can give her the faith to say, 'I know that my Redeemer lives.' That's the message people like your roommate are hungry to hear. It's like Carl and me when the kids were younger. When we had our fights and disagreements, don't you think we wanted to shut the door and keep our kids from seeing us at our ugliest? But we made it a point not to do that. We didn't want them to grow up believing the lie that marriage is easy. No, we fought in front of the kids, and things could get pretty heated at times. But we did that to teach our children that a godly couple can have their disagreements and afterwards still show love to each other, still respect one another. It's the same thing when we're witnessing. If our goal is to make people think that Christians never struggle, we're just setting them up for failure. What would your roommate think if she became a Christian because she believed you had a perfect, struggle-free life and wanted that for herself? Then, when she faces trials of her own, she'd feel like God abandoned her. So instead, you show her what it means to suffer and still have hope, to go through the valley of the shadow of death but know that the good Shepherd is right there, comforting you with his rod, guiding you with his staff. That's the kind of witness people today need to see."

She reached out and tucked a strand of loose hair behind Kennedy's ear. "We should never try to do God a favor by hiding our weaknesses. Don't hide your struggles. Just ask God to use them to show others his glory. Does that make sense?"

Kennedy nodded, and Sandy placed some more fruit on her plate as the door to the garage flung open.

"Did you miss me?" Carl brandished a smile and waved Kennedy's cell phone in one hand. He sat down at the head of the table. "This smells delicious. Pass me that fruit plate. I'm famished."

CHAPTER 23

Half an hour and two more banana muffins later, Kennedy's body reminded her how exhausted she was from the events of the past twenty-four hours. She hadn't thought until now about any of the toiletries she'd need, but Sandy always kept extra nightclothes and toothbrushes ready for occasions just like this.

"You sure you don't want some help cleaning up the dishes?" Kennedy asked.

"Just leave them," Sandy answered. "I'll get to them in the morning."

If she knew anything about Sandy, she was certain those dishes would be clean and dry in the dishwasher well before sunrise.

Sandy got up from the table. "I think I saved your toothbrush from last time. Let me go have a look." She started to bustle down the hall and stopped. "Oh, I almost forgot! Carl, do you have your note ready? We can ask Kennedy to do the picture tonight."

He scooted his chair back. "I've got it in the den. I'll go grab it."

Kennedy watched him hurry out of the dining room. "What note?"

"It's something we started last week when we first got matched with Woong from the South Korean orphanage. Carl and I made the decision that we'd write him a note each day until he comes home and take a picture of us holding it. It might not be much, but we wanted him to understand how much we loved him even before we met him face to face."

Kennedy figured that any orphan lucky enough to get paired up with the Lindgrens was one of the most blessed kids alive. "That's a really sweet idea."

"So, Carl's gonna grab his camera, and do you mind taking the picture for us? Otherwise, he'll have to fiddle with the timer, and half the time it goes off too early. I swear we could make a collection of all the pictures of Carl's backside to give to Woong."

Carl scurried in carrying a dry-erase board. "It's my night to do the message, right, babe?"

"Yeah. I thought you said you already wrote it." Sandy was repositioning photographs and homemade crafts on the mantle. "Come stand right here, Kennedy. We haven't gotten a shot by the fireplace in a little while." She frowned at Carl. "Weren't you wearing that last night?"

He glanced down at himself. "No, that was my other red shirt. This one's different."

"You sure?"

"Yeah." He reached into his pocket. "Now here you go. This camera ... Wait, where is it?"

Sandy rolled her eyes. "You lost it again?" She turned to Kennedy. "I swear, if Woong knew how much hassle we go through just to get him ..."

"I'm the one who said a ten-year-old boy ain't gonna care if he gets a picture every day," Carl countered. "It's not like he's going to pull out a magnifying glass and read each single date ..."

"It's the principle of the thing. We want him to know ..."

Kennedy grabbed her cell. "How about I take it on my phone and I'll just send it as an attachment to your email or something? Would that work?"

Carl lifted his eyebrows. "You can do that?"

"Yeah." She opened her camera app. "Are you guys ready?"

"I think so."

Sandy nudged Carl again. "You forgot the whiteboard."

"Oh, yeah."

Once everything was in place, Kennedy tried to take the shot.

"What was that beep?" Sandy asked. "Was that the picture? Do you want to take another one just to be sure?"

Kennedy frowned at her screen. "No, it's this phone. It's gotten low on memory. Hold on. I have to delete a few pictures, and then I'll try again." She sighed as she went into her gallery. For five minutes, maybe more, she had gone without thinking about Reuben, about the way her stupid phone's lousy memory was the reason he was spending the night in jail. She really should take those old lab photos and delete them all. It's not like ...

She froze.

"What is it, dear?" Sandy asked.

"Just give the girl a minute to do what she's gotta do."

Kennedy felt the blood rush from her head down to the finger that stood poised over her screen. Could it really be ...?

"Hold on."

Sandy hurried and stared over her shoulder. "What's the matter, sweetie? Is your battery dying?"

"No, it's not that. It's ..."

She wouldn't allow herself to hope. She couldn't. Her phone had said the memory was full. Why hadn't she thought to go into her photo album in the first place? Was it right there?

"Precious, is everything all right?"

"Give the girl some space, woman," Carl boomed without losing his good-natured tone.

Kennedy's finger was surprisingly calm as she selected the recording. It started to play. She glanced up at the Lindgrens. "I think I found the video that will get Reuben out of jail."

CHAPTER 24

Kennedy lost track of how many times she and the Lindgrens watched the video. It wasn't the full encounter, but it was enough. The phone's memory reached its max right after the cop knocked Reuben to the ground. It was enough to show Reuben hadn't instigated anything. Enough to exonerate him. Kennedy couldn't decide if she was more relieved to finally have the proof or mad at herself for not discovering it sooner.

Well, there was no way they would hold Reuben in jail for long, not with information like this. Now, the only question was who she should give it to. She tried calling her dad, but no one picked up either at the office or at home. She sent him an email and asked for the full name of his lawyer friend after a Google search showed at least twenty-seven attorneys in the greater Boston area called Jefferson.

"You know it's late, don't you?" Carl asked as she stared at her phone. "Even if the right people got a hold of this, Reuben won't be getting out tonight."

"Carl's right, hon." Sandy rubbed Kennedy's shoulders. "You can always wake up first thing tomorrow and then decide what to do. These things always seem to make more sense once you've had a good night's sleep."

A good night's sleep? Didn't they know, couldn't they understand that she had been begging God for the chance to get her hands on something like this, verifiable proof that Reuben was innocent? And now they were telling her to go to sleep and wait for morning?

"I'm not an expert in these things," Carl said, "but I know your dad pretty well, and I'm guessing he'd advise you to talk with Reuben's lawyer before you do anything else."

Carl was right, at least the part about that being what her dad would say.

Sandy took her by the arm. "If you come with me by the bathroom, sweetheart, I'll get you your toothbrush and some pajamas."

"We still need to take that picture for Woong," Carl reminded her.

"We don't need to keep Kennedy up for that. We can use the timer on your camera like usual."

Carl stood up with a groan. "Guess that means I better find it." He tousled Kennedy's hair affectionately. "Good night, kiddo. I hope you sleep well."

Kennedy thanked him again for letting her stay over and followed Sandy toward the bathroom. Once she was washed and dressed and alone in the Lindgrens' familiar guestroom, she turned on her phone and watched the video one more time. All her muscles were quivering, but now it was from excitement and not from fear. Reuben would be released. He would be just fine. Life could go on as normal. Hopefully, even better than normal, because Kennedy had already decided that once he got out, she wasn't going to take his friendship for granted anymore. She wasn't going to bide her time, wait to see what the future might bring, and spend her life wondering if things could have been different if she'd had the courage to confess her feelings. Maybe by this time tomorrow, she'd be with Reuben. Maybe by this time tomorrow, he'd know. She thought about the Bible verse that God works all things together for good for those who love him. Maybe that was what this was all about. Maybe God allowed Reuben to get arrested, knowing that this one night with him in jail would be enough to make Kennedy realize that she'd be the biggest fool in Massachusetts if she didn't tell him the truth.

The whole truth.

It would be scary, but hadn't her therapist told her it was time to take baby steps out of her comfort zone? Hadn't

Sandy just spent half an hour assuring Kennedy it was ok to feel inadequate, it was ok to feel weak? A cross-stitched verse that hung in the Lindgrens' dining room flitted through her mind: *Weeping may remain for a night, but rejoicing comes in the morning.* Maybe Carl and Sandy were right. Maybe she should try to sleep, get a hold of her dad first thing in the morning, find a way to get the video to Reuben's attorney. Weren't there verses in Proverbs that talked about patience being the wisest course of action? That's what her mom had told her growing up, at least. You regretted rushing into things more often than you'd ever regret waiting.

She lay down, relishing how much more comfortable the Lindgrens' bed was compared to her dorm mattress. If she didn't need access to the college library at all hours of the day and night, she might even be tempted to offer to pay Carl and Sandy room and board to stay here. At the very least, it was the perfect reprieve for a Friday night, a night that had started out disastrous but left Kennedy filled with hope. She wished she could catch this blissful feeling in a lab flask, close it up with a rubber stopper, and let it diffuse into her system whenever she needed.

Hope. One of God's most precious gifts for his children. She was ashamed at how she doubted him earlier, ashamed of how quickly she threw away her faith, when all this time, he knew that the video she needed and the proof she'd been begging for were right there on her phone. Maybe this was all God's way of bringing her and Reuben together.

Together. Another beautiful word, just like hope. Together ...

She had just allowed her mind to drift off into that first stage of drowsy sleep with its long, alpha brain waves when her phone rang.

Willow.

Was she still at the protest? How could Kennedy have forgotten to call her?

"Hello?" She tried to talk quietly in case Carl and Sandy were already in bed.

"Hey, sorry we lost you. Othello and I are going to stay out for a while, but do you want me to take you back to campus first?"

"No, that's ok. I forgot to text you earlier. I ran into my pastor and got a ride with him. I'll be staying at his place tonight."

"Nothing kinky, right?" Willow teased.

Kennedy ignored the remark. "How was the rest of the vigil?"

She had to strain to hear over all the background noise. "It's still going on, actually. They're on the third band doing a Beatles cover, so I'm out of here."

"Glad I didn't miss much, then. But hey, really good news. I found the video I thought I'd lost on my phone. It didn't get everything, but it was recording for over two minutes before the memory ran out. I'm gonna find a way to get it to Reuben's lawyer in the morning."

"What's that?" Willow was shouting now. "I didn't hear that last part. You said something about your phone?"

"I'll just text you." She didn't want to raise her voice and bother Carl and Sandy.

"Ok, I can't hear you too good, so just call or text me if you need something. Otherwise I'll see you back on campus."

Kennedy said goodbye even though she couldn't be certain Willow heard it. She opened up her text messages and sent a quick note about the video.

I want to see it! Willow immediately responded.

The video file was too large to text, so she sent it as an email attachment, grateful to have someone else to share the good news with.

Yes, things had taken a positive turn. A very positive turn.

Kennedy figured she was about to get the best sleep she'd had in weeks.

CHAPTER 25

"Do you think we should wake her up?"

"I'm not sure. We could wait."

Carl and Sandy's words slipped through the fog of Kennedy's heavy sleep.

"She's gonna find out eventually. It might be best if she hears it from us."

"I know, I just wish the little lamb could have a few more minutes to rest. She was so tired last night."

Kennedy rubbed her eyes. She always felt so disoriented when she woke up at the Lindgrens', as if her body wasn't accustomed to a real mattress and was looking for the hard, cardboard-like substitute from her dorm room.

"I think we should tell her ourselves. Otherwise she might see the news on her phone or something."

"You're probably right. I just wish ..." Sandy didn't finish her thought. Kennedy's brain was only half awake, like her computer after she turned it on but had to wait for all her programs to load. What were they talking about? What news did they have for her?

Something about Reuben?

A small knock on the guest room door. Timid. Almost apologetic.

"Come in."

Sandy with her long brown hair out of its normal French brain. A frown on her usually cheerful face. Dark lines under her eyes. Had she slept at all?

Carl muttering something as he passed down the hall. Apparently, this was women's business. So it was Reuben, then. Had something happened to him? Had he been attacked in jail?

Please, God. No.

That giant swell of hope she'd experienced last night, that first taste of true joy she'd felt in weeks, came crashing down around her. Something was wrong. Sandy's face was pale. Kennedy knew her psyche wasn't strong enough for another crisis. Her lungs pulled tight in her chest.

Sandy sat down gingerly on the edge of the bed and placed her hand on Kennedy's knee. "Something happened last night."

Time distorted itself. How could the theory of relativity explain this kind of phenomenon? How could Einstein, brilliant as he was, rationalize the way Kennedy found herself pulled out of normal temporal reality until everything was slow? Viscous. Even her body's autonomic functions, the pounding of her pulse in her ears, decelerated inexplicably.

Sandy took in a deep breath. It was the same look a nurse would give her patient before turning her over for a spinal tap.

Where was that hope? Where was that peace now?

"It's about that video," Sandy began. Even her voice sounded lower, warped somehow. Was Kennedy ill? Was her brain sick? Had she fallen victim to some sort of bizarre sensory disorder that left her feeling so detached? Disoriented?

Sandy stared at her lap. Her hair was beautiful. Silky. Light brown with respectable hints of long, gray streaks. Why didn't she wear it down more?

"I need to ask you something," Sandy began. Kennedy made a note that when she was a doctor delivering a fatal prognosis, she would offer the bad news in a single sentence. No lengthy prefaces. No chitchat to decrease the shock. It was easier that way. Easier to know the truth and confront it than deal with the dreadful uncertainty.

Sandy made an apologetic sound in the back of her throat. "Did you send the video to anyone last night before you went to bed?"

"I showed it to Willow. My roommate. I was excited that we … I wanted her to see …" Kennedy stopped fumbling over her words and asked simply, "What happened?"

"We don't know how, but the media got hold of it. Last night before Carl and I went to sleep. There was a …"

Kennedy watched Sandy's throat muscles constrict.

"Once the video got out, people were even more upset, more angry about what happened to your friend. There was an incident last night at the vigil." She avoided Kennedy's eyes.

An incident? What did that mean? What was Sandy saying?

"Is Reuben ok?" Did Sandy know how Kennedy felt? Did she guess how important Reuben was to her? If this was a little schoolgirl crush, she imagined Sandy would want to talk about it for hours over tea and homemade biscotti, but so far that particular subject had never been broached.

"Reuben's fine, dear." For the first time that morning, Sandy smiled.

Kennedy let her muscles relax. The iron sheath that had encased her rib cage loosened itself, and she could breathe easier.

As quickly as it came, however, Sandy's smile faded. "There was a problem at the courthouse, though." She winced as though the words were painful to speak. "A riot."

Kennedy felt guilty for feeling more relief than horror. Relief that Reuben was still safe. Relief that the public was on her side. The police would have to let Reuben free now.

Sandy let out a small choking sound, and Kennedy was startled to see tears streak down her cheeks. Her pulse quickened. How bad of a riot could it have been?

"Was anyone injured?" she asked and suddenly remembered Willow. Had she been there? Had she shared the video with Othello's crowd at the courthouse and stayed to watch the drama unfold? Kennedy was selfish to only worry about Reuben at a time like this. What about her roommate?

Sandy was shaking her head. "Only one injury." Her voice tightened. "A little baby."

Kennedy was certain she had misheard. What kind of a parent would bring a baby to an event like that? And what kind of criminals ...

She froze, remembering the young mother who had asked if she needed help. The baby in the sling. Maybe it wasn't so impossible, after all. Why shouldn't a parent attend a prayer vigil with a small child? It's something Kennedy's parents might have done when she was little.

Kennedy didn't trust her voice to get out the next question. Wasn't sure she wanted to know the answer. "Did the baby ..." No, that's not what she wanted to say. "Was it very serious?"

Sandy sniffed. "We don't know yet. She's at the Children's Hospital at Providence now."

"What happened?"

"It sounds like the mom was running to get away when the violence broke out and tripped. The baby was in a front pack, and …"

"Is she going to be ok?" Kennedy wished she could hold audience with God if only for a few minutes. Ask him why he would allow something so horrible to happen. Why he would harm such a young and innocent life for no apparent reason.

Sandy shook her head. "I don't know. I just don't know." She was gripping Kennedy's hand.

"I'm sorry," Kennedy whispered.

Sandy's head shot up. "Whatever for, sweetheart?"

"I shouldn't have sent the video. Should have told Willow to keep it private."

Horror, the full realization of what she had done, sank into Kennedy's being little by little, like droplets of groundwater percolating down through layers of soil and gravel.

Sandy stretched out her arms and wrapped her in a hug. "It's not your fault, honey. Nobody would ever wish something like that to happen to a little baby. It's not your fault," she repeated, but Kennedy had a hard time listening through her tears.

CHAPTER 26

Kennedy texted Willow as soon as Sandy left. She doubted her roommate would be awake at nine on a Saturday morning, but she had to make sure her friend was safe. Willow replied right away, apologizing for the video leak.

I only shared it with Othello so he could see what was happening. I didn't know he was going to pass it on.

Kennedy was just glad to know Willow was safe. According to her text, Willow had sensed the tensions rising and left before the real violence erupted. Othello had stuck around with his friends, and Willow hadn't heard from him yet.

I'm sure he's fine, Kennedy assured her. After all, the only reported injury was that little baby.

The Lindgrens spent the morning keeping Kennedy distracted. As soon as Kennedy got out of bed, Sandy put her to work making a hearty brunch. Saturday morning brunch had been a regular custom in Kennedy's family for as long as she could remember, and she wondered if Sandy knew about their tradition. It took over an hour and a half to get everything baked and cooked. Then while Sandy set the table, Kennedy taught Carl how to use the timer on his camera properly so they could take their pictures for Woong more easily.

Breakfast at the Lindgrens' involved more than just sitting around the table, sipping fresh coffee, and stuffing yourself into a gluttonous stupor. Carl started each day with morning devotions, which he read from a Charles Spurgeon book Kennedy had never heard of before meeting the Lindgrens. Then, Sandy pulled out her prayer box, a cutely painted recipe holder with index cards arranged by category. Kennedy still hadn't figured the system out entirely, but there were certain people the Lindgrens prayed for every day, and others they prayed for on a weekly or monthly basis. After prayers, Carl passed Kennedy his old Bible so she could participate in the reading for the day. He and Sandy made their way through the Bible once a year, and Kennedy read a chapter from Joshua before passing it back to Carl to finish.

After Sandy refilled the coffee mugs and set another round of blueberry pancakes on the table, she took out a journal with a bright tulip pattern on the front.

"So last year at this time," she said, slipping on her pair of reading glasses, "we were praying for Blessing to have favor in her job situation at the bank, and we were asking God for a better daycare situation for Tyson that would be closer to her work." She took a pencil and drew two lines across the page. "God certainly took care of both of those worries, didn't he?"

Carl nodded back with a smile.

Sandy read through the rest of that page, striking out the requests that had already been answered and stopping to pray for those that hadn't yet come to pass. She flowed ceaselessly from her conversation with Carl and Kennedy into prayer and back again, so Kennedy half expected to see Jesus sitting in one of the empty chairs around the table. When she was finished, Sandy flipped ahead in her journal and wrote the day's date in her flowing cursive handwriting. "So of course, we're praying for Reuben's release and that poor little baby who was hurt. What else?"

By the time they finished breakfast devotions, Carl excused himself to get some work done at the church office. "Do you want me to give you a ride back to your dorm?" he asked Kennedy.

"If you don't mind." As restful as her time at the Lindgrens' had been, she knew she had to go back. If Reuben wasn't released over the weekend, he would definitely be freed after his arraignment Monday morning. Until then,

Kennedy had to work on their lab report on her own. She also needed to start some research for a Roald Dahl paper for her children's literature class.

Sandy packed the brunch leftovers into various sized Tupperware and set them in a canvas bag for Kennedy to take back to campus. Sandy was clearing the table and Carl was hunting for his missing sermon notes when Kennedy's phone rang. She didn't recognize the number but wasn't about to miss a chance to talk to Reuben. Did he even know about the video? Did he know he was going to be released? Had he heard about the riots and the price paid for justice?

"Hello?" Kennedy made her way into the Lindgrens' guest bedroom for privacy.

"I'm looking for a Miss Kennedy Stern."

Kennedy shut the door behind her. "This is she. What can I do for you?"

"So where is this interview you're going to?" Carl asked as he drove Kennedy back to Harvard.

"Somewhere off the Orange Line." Kennedy fidgeted with her seatbelt and glanced at the dashboard clock. If she got back to her dorm in fifteen minutes, she'd have a little less than half an hour to change her clothes and get ready before she had to catch the T to Tufts.

"And who is this woman who called you?"

"Her name's Diane Fil-something. She's got a show on Channel 2."

Carl frowned. "Have you researched her background or anything?"

Kennedy wasn't surprised that her dad and Carl had been such good friends in college. In many ways, they were exactly like each other.

"She just said she wanted to talk to me about the video, get my side of the story."

"Yeah, I'm sure that's what she said," Carl muttered as he exited off the freeway. "I just want you to be careful. These news anchors, they don't care about you. In most cases, they don't even care about victims or civil liberties. You know what they care about? Ratings. So the more they can shock the audience, the better."

"This should be pretty straightforward." Kennedy didn't know why she should have to defend herself or her choices all of a sudden. "She said they'll play the video clip, I'll answer a few questions about when we got pulled over, and they'll cut to a commercial or something. I don't think it will be too hard."

"That's because you're a decent kid with nothing to hide," Carl explained. "But you better believe me, if you had a skeleton in your closet, it's people like this Diane What's-Her-Name who'd gamble away their grandmother's soul to be the first to break the story." He patted her knee. "I'm sorry. I shouldn't be so negative. I hope you have a really good interview. Just be careful, ok?"

"Thanks."

They drove a while in silence. Carl tuned his car radio to some conservative talk show but punched it off as soon as the host mentioned the riot at the courthouse. So far, Kennedy had resisted the morbid urge to look up footage from the event. She didn't know how much damage had been done, but the streets seemed relatively calm for the middle of a Saturday. Were people staying home? Did the police think the riots would get worse?

Carl pulled his Honda up to a curb near Harvard Square. "See you at church tomorrow?"

"If I get this lab report done by then," Kennedy answered. She slung her new canvas bag laden with leftovers on her shoulder, waved goodbye, and shut the door. She pulled her phone out of her pocket to glance at the time as Carl pulled away. If she hurried, she might even have time to wash her hair before she went on TV.

CHAPTER 27

Kennedy would have never guessed how much work went into preparing for a television interview. She arrived at the Channel 2 building ten minutes late and was immediately whisked into a makeup chair. While two different attendants muttered and frowned and fawned over her, Diane Fiddlestein's assistant barraged Kennedy with questions on every topic, from her time in China to her parents' missionary work, which Kennedy had to explain was a taboo subject due to her parents' sensitive relationship with the Chinese government. He asked her about her abduction last fall, and Kennedy's cheeks burned when she explained to him she still had flashbacks from the event and would prefer not to discuss it on live television. He assured her he would pass the message on to Miss Fiddlestein and then interrogated her about Reuben, the nature of their relationship, what part of Kenya he was from, what kind of grades he got.

"Is she really going to ask all this during the interview?" Kennedy had lost track of the time but was pretty sure they'd been talking for over half an hour when the interview was only scheduled to last about five minutes.

The assistant explained that this was common procedure. While a hair designer slathered Kennedy with hairspray, the assistant told her where to find bottled water or tea while she waited for the interview.

Apparently, she hadn't needed to be so preoccupied with being late, since she ended up with about forty-five minutes to wait behind the set for her turn. She was glad she had brought a book with her and found that *The Trumpet of the Swan*, which was on the suggested reading list for her children's literature course, was the perfect way to calm her nerves. Carl's warning about television anchors buzzed in the back of her head like an annoying mosquito, so she focused instead on the world of Louis, a swan who longed to share his voice with the world.

During a commercial break, while Diane Fiddlestein yelled at the teleprompter operator for some error he insisted he had no control over, her assistant led Kennedy to a beige loveseat.

"Your interview starts in two minutes. Can I get you one last drink of water?"

Kennedy shook her head, and he went on to summarize all the rules he'd already gone over before: speak clearly, ignore the camera, maintain eye contact with Diane, and stay completely on topic. Kennedy figured if she could multitask the procedure for a spectrophotometric determination experiment in the lab, she could make it through a five-minute interview.

"All right," someone in a headset called out. "We're up."

·Kennedy found it a little strange that this would actually be her first conversation with Diane, but she was more concerned about proving Reuben's innocence than about how forced and contrived their meeting felt.

The man in the headphones held up his fingers and yelled out the countdown. They were on live TV.

The segment started with a few short snippets from Kennedy's encounter with Bow Legs. She was glad they showed it off-screen so she didn't have to watch it herself. She rubbed her clammy hands on her fitted wool slacks and tried to focus on long, controlled breathing. Five minutes. That's all this was. Five minutes for Reuben. She could do this.

She was so focused on stuffing her anxiety into one small enclosed place in the center of her gut that she wasn't paying attention to Diane Fiddlestein's smiley introduction. Fortunately, after Diane thanked her for being on the show, Kennedy's brain automatically kicked in with the expected exchange of pleasantries.

"So, Kennedy." Diane folded her hands in her lap. Kennedy wondered if there was a metal rod surgically plastered against her spine that allowed her to sit up so tall. Diane's smile was dazzlingly pretty, the dark red of her lips accentuating the perfect whiteness of her enamel, but there was a snakelike quality to her look that reminded Kennedy of the serpent witch in *The Silver Chair*. "Tell me," Diane began, "how did you feel when you learned that Reuben had been arrested last night?"

Kennedy was glad she hadn't asked about her encounter with the police. This was all about Reuben, after all. That's why she was here.

"I was upset, obviously. I knew Reuben hadn't done anything wrong, so I felt it was unfair when they took him away."

Took him away? Maybe she'd been spending too much time reading children's literature. It sounded like she had the vocabulary of a fourth grader.

"So tell us about the video we just watched," Diane went on. "I'm told the camera was hidden in your pocket?"

"Right. I turned it on when it looked like there might be some sort of confrontation. If things escalated, I wanted to have it on tape."

Diane nodded encouragingly, but her next question was

far blunter than the previous. "And why did you wait a whole day to bring the truth to light?"

"I thought my camera had malfunctioned. I got a message after the incident that said it was out of memory, so I ..."

"But obviously it wasn't if you had the recording after all."

"I only got the first few minutes," Kennedy explained. "The rest was ..."

Diane didn't let her finish. "And how did you feel when you learned that your video resulted in a riot that injured a seven-month-old baby?"

"I was devastated. I never wanted anything like that to ..."

"So, you'll be happy to learn the baby was released from Providence this afternoon?"

Kennedy felt like she was in one of Professor Adell's lab lectures, unable to keep up with the pace. "That's great."

Diane jumped in as soon as Kennedy paused for breath. "And Reuben, the young man who was arrested, how would you describe him?"

The only reason Kennedy agreed to this interview in the first place was for the chance to clear Reuben's name. She told Diane about how good of a student he was, how encouraging, how he always had kind words, how he loved his family back in Kenya.

The whole time she talked, Diane busied her fingers unfolding a piece of paper that seemed to have materialized from nowhere. She frowned. "It says here that your friend's father was involved in the administration of former Kenyan dictator Daniel arap Moi. What can you tell me about that?"

Kennedy knew hardly anything about Kenya's history or politics. She'd never heard the name Diane mentioned. Reuben's conversation about his family was almost entirely limited to his numerous sisters and their dozens of children. "I really couldn't say," she stammered.

"I also find myself wondering why Reuben was sent overseas for his college education?" Diane's perfect smile chilled Kennedy's spine like the White Witch's winter curse in *The Lion, the Witch, and the Wardrobe*.

"Well, Harvard's a good school with a great international reputation ..."

Diane was frowning at the piece of paper, not listening to Kennedy at all. "Is it possible that Reuben was sent to the States because people with his condition get better medical treatment here than they would in a Nairobi hospital?"

Kennedy wondered if something even as warm as Aslan's breath would be enough to melt the icicles that had attached themselves to her nerve endings. "What medical condition?"

Diane pointed at her piece of paper, even though it was too far away for Kennedy to read. "It says here that your friend was diagnosed as HIV-positive."

Kennedy's throat tightened. She threw a pleading look at Diane, who sat cold and frigid like Empress Jadis on her throne.

"I'm not sure that ... I don't think ..."

"So I guess he didn't tell you before you started dating him." Diane frowned in false sympathy, pouting at the camera. "Well, when you see him again, please wish him the best. You'll be happy to hear I just got word that his arraignment has been rescheduled for this afternoon. If all goes well for his case, you'll be together again tonight. Thanks so much for joining us today, and I wish you both well."

Kennedy was too stunned to leave her chair once they turned the cameras off. Somewhere in a different part of the studio, a weatherman cracked jokes about an early spring heat wave, but his words flowed past Kennedy like time and space zooming past Meg in *A Wrinkle in Time*.

Nobody, not a single one of the dozens of backstage assistants noticed her. She stood herself up, trying to find something to settle her thoughts on, a focal point to pull her out of her daze.

The next commercial break ushered in a cacophony of

noise and movement, and Kennedy half expected Diane Fiddlestein to reappear and apologize for making such a heinous joke on live television, but she was already behind her desk, sharing whispers with her co-host. Kennedy was surprised her legs could hold her weight, surprised her brain could still function.

Shouldn't the world have stopped turning? Shouldn't her entire nervous system have shut down?

She let herself out of the backstage area and followed the exit signs until she found the elevators that took her to the main level. She walked out of the lobby and found herself alone on the Boston curbside in a world that in a single instant had lost all sense of beauty, justice, or hope.

CHAPTER 28

By the time Kennedy got off the T and arrived back to campus, she had ignored calls from Carl and Sandy as well as three other numbers she didn't recognize before she turned her phone off.

As she walked to her dorm, she felt the stares of the students around her. Did they know? Could they guess?

It didn't make sense. Reuben with HIV? AIDS was one of those things like malaria — you learned about it, you knew it was bad, but you never expected someone you knew to actually have it.

She thought back to his brooding silences in spite of his otherwise cheerful, steady mood. His reluctance to take their story to the police department or the media. Had he known? Had he guessed the press would dig into his background?

Why hadn't he told her? Or had he tried? Was that the secret? It didn't have anything to do with Kennedy or any sort of romantic feelings at all. It was about his diagnosis.

She realized with irony that she wasn't suffering from

even a hint of anxiety. No clammy hands. No racing pulse. No constricting lungs. Just a heaviness, as if someone had replaced her bone marrow with molten lead. Everything seemed to ache, but she wasn't in pain anywhere.

HIV positive? How had he gotten it? How long had he known? Would things change now that the truth was out? Wouldn't they have to?

It wasn't fair. HIV didn't impact people like Reuben. Did it?

She thought back to all her interactions with him in the lab. She couldn't have gotten herself contaminated. It wasn't like catching a cold or anything.

She glanced at her silenced phone, wishing it weren't the middle of the night in Yanji. Who could she talk to about this? Who could she turn to? She had already spent too much time at the Lindgrens' this weekend. Besides, Carl had tried to warn her before she appeared on that stupid interview in the first place. Why hadn't she listened to him?

And what about Dominic the chaplain? Hadn't he said Reuben had his reasons for wanting to avoid public scrutiny? Had Reuben told him — Dominic, a perfect stranger — before he told his best friend? Had Dominic bewitched him with his powerful prayers as well?

She thought back over every conversation with Reuben,

every trip off campus, every late night in the library, every meal together in the student union. Had he ever hinted? Ever come close to telling the truth?

Did she even know him anymore?

She reached her dorm and found her room empty. Good. She didn't have the energy to deal with Willow. She didn't even have the energy to deal with her own chaotic emotions. Why couldn't God have invented a Pensieve like in the J. K. Rowling books, a bowl she could dump her thoughts into and pull them out one by one to examine them until they were organized? Under control.

She slumped onto her bed. Would she ever feel joy again? They had moved Reuben's arraignment to this afternoon. He could be home by tonight. They could spend tomorrow working on their lab and hand it in first thing Monday. But would it ever be the same? Would it ever feel like it had before?

She squeezed silent tears from the corners of her eyes. Why hadn't he told her? And what would happen now?

The door opened slowly, and Kennedy wished she had gotten herself under the blankets. If she had to pretend to be asleep, she'd at least rather be comfortable.

"Hey." Willow's greeting sounded like an apology. "You ok?"

In all the history of the world, had a dumber question ever been asked? Or was it possible Willow didn't know? Possible she hadn't heard.

"I thought you'd be down at the courthouse. Didn't you get my text? The arraignment's in less than an hour."

"I'm not going," Kennedy mumbled.

Willow loosened her scarf and sat on the edge of Kennedy's bed. "Did something happen?"

"Reuben has AIDS." Never in her entire life had Kennedy expected to string those three words together. Why did God create the world to be so full of suffering? So full of horror?

"What?"

"Well, he's got HIV at least."

"How do you know? Did he tell you?"

"It was on the news." She didn't have the heart to tell Willow about the interview. She wished she could wrap herself up like the Very Hungry Caterpillar in its chrysalis and hide out there until she was ready to face the world with wings.

With hope.

With beauty.

Willow rubbed Kennedy's back. "Are you worried? Did you forget to use condoms or anything?"

Kennedy shook her head, no longer surprised at Willow's ingrained belief that it was impossible to be both a college student and a virgin at the same time.

"Well, that's something to be thankful for." She got up. "Want some tea?"

No. She didn't want anything. Except maybe a heavy dose of barbiturates so she could put herself into a medically induced coma until she was thirty and had life figured out.

Willow slipped on some of her hand-designed bangle bracelets. "I'm really sorry. For both of you."

Kennedy clenched her jaw shut. If Willow kept talking, she'd have to scream to drown the sound out.

"I really think you should come to the arraignment." Willow squirted some mousse into her palm and scrunched it through her hair. "He's going to get released, you know."

Kennedy figured that Willow was right. But what if he didn't? What if there was another riot? Another hurt kid? No, a world where God allowed those kinds of tragedies to run rampant wasn't a kind of world Kennedy wanted to live in anymore.

She held her breath, slightly frightened by the intensity of her emotions. Should she call the campus psychologist? Or maybe she was overreacting. It was normal to feel this way. Who wouldn't be a little down after everything Kennedy'd been through?

Willow slipped on her high-heeled black boots. All Kennedy could think of was how hard it would be for Willow to run away if more violence broke out at the courthouse.

"I'm gonna get my car. If you change your mind in the next few minutes, call me and I'll swing by and pick you up."

Kennedy was too exhausted to say thank you and nodded instead.

"It's going to be all right." Willow sounded so convinced. Maybe that's why she was the theater major. "Everything will work itself out in the end."

CHAPTER 29

Ten or fifteen minutes after Willow left, Kennedy still hadn't moved. She knew pretty soon she would jump online to see if the news covered Reuben's arraignment. But what if the judge didn't dismiss the case like everyone was expecting? What if Reuben would have to wait in jail for weeks or months before his trial, or what if the judge decided to deport him right then? She wished her dad had given her the full name of his lawyer friend. She had so many questions for him.

And what would happen if they didn't let Reuben go? People had been upset enough last night. What would they do today? The thought of anyone else getting hurt made her stomach contents curdle. Maybe she should buy herself some Tums.

She avoided her computer for as long as she could. Willow was probably halfway to the courthouse by the time she finally dragged herself out of bed to sit down at her desk. She waited for everything to start up and wondered if she was doing the right thing. Should she just wait? Willow or one of the Lindgrens would let her know once the decision was made, right?

Instead of jumping on the internet right away, she opened the Excel file that had the results from her most recent lab. She still had to manipulate some of the data before she could graph the results. It was a simple task, really, something she could have done in a minute or two on a good day. She botched it up three different times before she gave up.

She moved her cursor to open up the web but paused before clicking. No. She wasn't ready. She hadn't even seen the riot last night, but images of angry protesters clashing with police crept uninvited through her cerebral cortex. She wondered if Dominic had been there when the violence erupted. Did chaplains get involved in things like riots? She didn't even know if he carried a gun.

She stared at the time. The arraignment wouldn't start for a few more minutes. She had no idea how long the whole thing would last. She had no idea when the judge would reach a decision. How long would it take for him to dismiss the case and set Reuben free? How long would Kennedy have to wait in the meantime, wondering, fearful?

She turned her phone back on. Maybe she'd regret her decision. Maybe not. She found the contact she was looking for and waited for the call to go through.

"Hello?"

"Hi, I hate to bother you, but I was wondering if you'd come with me to the courthouse downtown."

"I'm so glad you called, sweetie."

Kennedy had lost track of how many times Sandy had said the exact same thing since she picked her up from Harvard in the Lindgrens' maroon Honda.

"I was just telling Carl I hoped you weren't alone. It can take a lot of courage asking for help. I'm really proud of you."

Kennedy hadn't thought about it in those terms. Honestly, she didn't think courage had much to do with it. She had just been too scared to wait alone to hear the results.

Sandy turned down her praise and worship CD. "I saw your interview, by the way. I was so sorry to hear about Reuben."

Kennedy already hated the way people like Sandy and Willow tiptoed around the subject. They treated it as though it was so private, so painful to mention, yet Diane Fiddlestein had broadcast the horrible, ugly truth to the entire world.

"I assume you didn't know before today?" Sandy said with a hint of a question in her tone.

"No." As soon as she called Sandy to ask her for a ride, she knew this conversation would come up.

"It must have hit you as quite a shock."

Kennedy hated those kinds of clichés. *Quite a shock.* What else was it supposed to be when you found out your best friend had contracted one of history's most horrific viruses?

"I hate to have to ask this, sweetie." Sandy cleared her throat. "But I know how college students these days are, and I know that even good Christian kids make mistakes."

Kennedy rolled her eyes when she realized what was coming next.

"You and Reuben weren't ever ... intimate, were you?"

Kennedy shook her head. Why was that everybody's first concern? And why was everyone so relieved to find out that Kennedy and Reuben hadn't been sleeping together? That still didn't change the fact that one day — whether next month or in five or ten years — he was going to die a hideous, undignified death.

"Well, I'm sorry I had to ask, but you know ..." Her voice died out. "It's not the kind of thing you catch from kissing as far as I understand."

"We don't do any of that," Kennedy replied sullenly.

"Well, I knew you two are close, so I had to ask." Sandy patted her hand, and Kennedy guessed that Sandy was the more uncomfortable of the two right now.

"Do you like him?"

Kennedy didn't want to talk about it. Because if she talked about it, then she had to think about it. The more she thought about it, the more she realized there was no real solution.

"I mean as more than a friend," Sandy pressed. "You like him like that?"

"I've started to," Kennedy confessed.

Neither of them spoke. Kennedy wondered if Sandy had already examined the different options and found each of them just as impossible as Kennedy had. It was stupid to end a friendship over something like HIV. It's not like she could catch it standing next to him for too long in the lab. But to continue on in a perfectly platonic relationship with him, Kennedy would have to deny the growing part of her heart that wanted more. That wanted something deeper. But how deep could it ever go? They could date as long as they kept their physical boundaries, but then what? You don't keep dating someone for the rest of your life. What kind of future did she and Reuben have to look forward to? What kind of ending could their story have besides tragedy and heartache?

"There was a time," Sandy began, "I was seeing two young men at once. Well, sort of. I'd been going steady with a doctor from Virginia for a few years by the time I met Carl. And well, things got more and more confusing from there. So I asked my grandpa about it. He was blind by then. Senile, too. Didn't know what a ruckus I'd caused in the family by even thinking about dating a black man. I just told him there were two men, didn't say anything about their skin color or nothing like that. But I asked him what he thought I should do, and you know what he said? He said the best decision he'd ever made in life was to marry his best friend. So that's what I did, too."

It was a nice story, one that a week ago might have given Kennedy a warm, gushy feeling in her gut. "It's a little different when someone's so sick, you know."

Sandy didn't reply right away, and Kennedy felt guilty. What good was it making Sandy just as depressed as she was?

Sandy hummed along with the worship song for a few bars and then took a deep breath. "We took in a little foster baby once, Carl and I," she began. "Sweetest little thing you'd ever meet. Had a condition. I forget the name, had to do with amniotic something. A lot of birth defects. A lot.

Doctors suspected he had some genetic disorders, too, but they weren't able to check for those kind of things as well back then. So this little sweetheart, Spencer his name was, he had a lot of physical deformities. Internal problems, too. When he was born, the doctors thought he'd only last a month or two. It was too much for the birth parents to handle. They're fine people, I'm sure, but it was too heartbreaking for them. That's how we ended up welcoming little Spencer into our family.

"And you know what? It would have been easier for us if we never brought him home, easier emotionally as well as practically. I don't think I got a full night's sleep the entire time he was with us. The doctors told us he was going to die. One doctor even suggested we hold off on some of the medicine that was helping because it was only prolonging the inevitable. But you know what? That precious little child gave us seven months of joy. And when I say joy, I'm not pretending it was perfect and rosy. I'm not saying it was easy. I'm not saying our hearts didn't break, because they did. Every single day, my spirit just ripped in two when I held little Spencer and knew he only had such a short time with us. But you know what? That's what made having him in our home and in our lives so special. We didn't ask to fall in love with a sick little baby with a terminal diagnosis. We didn't ask to go through that valley of grief that stretched on for seven long months and then beyond that after he was gone. But believe me when I tell you that the time I had with Spencer was worth every second of heartache, and if I had the choice, I'd do it all over again."

Kennedy knew that only loosely veiled behind Sandy's words were wisdom and admonitions she could take to heart, but she wasn't ready to think in those terms yet. Sandy seemed to sense she had said enough, because she squeezed Kennedy's hand and turned the music back up.

They were closer to the courthouse now. Kennedy's breath grew shorter with each block they passed. There was some kind of tangible discontent in the air. Fear and anger. Or was that just her imagination?

Police in riot gear had formed perimeters in several locations. Kennedy sat paralyzed in her passenger seat. Sandy held her sweaty hand in hers.

"Don't worry, hon." She pointed. "See those people?" She rolled down her window. "Hear that noise? They're clapping. I think it's good news." She glanced from one side of the road to the other. "Now, I just wonder where I can find a place to park."

At the exact same moment, the victorious roar of the crowd jumped at least twenty or thirty decibels.

"What's going on?" Sandy asked, but Kennedy didn't have the breath to answer. When the Honda pulled up to a stop sign, Kennedy jumped out and started sprinting. Her heart, already overworked from anxiety, swelled to near-bursting capacity.

He was there at the top of the courthouse steps, smiling sheepishly at the thunderous crowd.

She didn't pause as she passed the police line. Hardly slowed down as she maneuvered her way through the congested sidewalks. Raced to the steps of the courthouse and took them two at a time.

She saw the spark in his eyes the moment he recognized her. Saw the joy.

The din on the streets grew even louder when he rushed down the steps to meet her. They hugged. Kennedy was crying, but it wasn't the suffocating sobs like what gripped her in the worst of her panic attacks.

"I'm so glad to see you." Reuben held her close.

Kennedy didn't have the voice to respond. She had spent nearly all semester in agonizing introspection, asking herself if she loved Reuben.

Tonight, she had her answer.

CHAPTER 30

"Ok, so what's the big surprise?" Kennedy asked. "Are we going to shop for books at Common Treasures?"

As hard as he tried, Reuben couldn't hide his smile. "Nope. Well, maybe, but we don't have time for that yet."

Kennedy glanced around at the lazy Sunday afternoon traffic, searching for clues. She and Reuben had always joked about riding the swan boats in Boston Common, but that was expensive. After her dad paid for Reuben's lawyer fees, Kennedy wasn't going to ask for anything extra for at least another month. And Reuben wasn't the type to have extra cash on hand. So where was he taking her?

Last night after his release, they'd been so tired they ate dinner together in the student union and then returned to their dorms where Kennedy slept for eleven hours straight. Today he'd told her to meet him at the library after lunch, but when she showed up with her calculus text and lab notebook, he made her take it back to her room. That's when he said he had a surprise for her off campus.

They still hadn't talked about much else besides school since his release. In some ways, they were like two kids at the end of summer vacation, not willing to acknowledge the obvious signs of autumn in the air.

They would have to talk. Soon. But neither of them was ready yet.

Once she heard about his diagnosis, Kennedy had been so terrified. So worried that even if Reuben was released from jail, things could never be the same between them. There would be long periods of awkwardness. Painful silences.

She had been wrong.

Delightfully wrong.

Reuben held her hand as they sprinted across the street. Would she ever forget the way his fingers felt interlaced with hers? Somewhere in the back of her head, she felt she was growing to understand Sandy's story about the little baby Spencer they cared for. She wasn't willing to admit it, wasn't willing to use terms like *dying* yet, but the story implanted itself to a safe spot in her memory banks, ready for her to pull out and examine when the time was right.

They sped by Common Treasures, the antique bookstore where they could lose themselves for hours wandering through old volumes and early editions of their favorite stories. Kennedy was laughing even though she didn't know what was so funny.

Reuben stopped in front of the Boston Opera House. "Here we are."

"What's this?" she asked.

Reuben slipped in line for call waiting. "Mr. Jefferson said your dad overpaid him. Said the case wasn't as hard as he'd originally planned once you found that video. So he gave me a check, said your dad would want us to do something fun together." He stepped up to the counter. "Two tickets for *Aida*. It's under the name Reuben Murunga."

"Really?" Kennedy squealed but wasn't embarrassed.

Reuben grinned and passed her a ticket. "I have a feeling we've earned this."

Kennedy had grown up seeing musicals in Manhattan — *Phantom, Les Mis, Cats*. Even after her family moved to Yanji, her mom would buy the DVD versions of the most popular shows and watch them with Kennedy on nights when her dad was working late. Kennedy knew musical theater had the power to impact your emotions, take you on a ride of thrills or excitement or joy. But she never knew it could do something like this.

She hadn't known much about *Aida* before the show came to Boston. She knew it was a love story set in ancient Egypt and that was about it. What she hadn't counted on was the sacrificial love shown between the two main characters — Aida, the Nubian princess who was willing to give up her relationship with her Egyptian captor in order to lead her people, and Radames, heir to Pharaoh's throne who forsook his birthright to help his beloved find freedom.

She assumed it would be a story of love fulfilled, but in reality it was the story of impossible relationships. In the final scene, both Aida and Radames were buried alive for their treason against Egypt. Was dying in the arms of your beloved more bearable than facing life without him?

As the curtain closed, she sat beside Reuben, acutely aware of his gentle expression and the tears on her own cheeks. It was stupid to cry. It was just a musical after all. Just a musical ...

She didn't talk on their way out of the theater. She didn't know what to say. She felt like a leaf, floating down a merciless current. The river forked just ahead, but she wouldn't know which route she'd take until it would be too late to ever go back.

CHAPTER 31

"That was a good show, wasn't it?" Reuben asked. They had stopped by Angelo's Pizza to grab a quick dinner before heading back to campus.

A good show? Kennedy wasn't sure that's what she'd call it. She needed more time to think through it all. Process everything she'd seen. Figure out what the musical was trying to say to her. She had this unshakeable sense that somewhere in Aida's tragic romance was a lesson, a warning meant specifically for her. Was she too stupid to discern what it was?

Or too scared?

Reuben ate surprisingly little. He reached across the table and took Kennedy's hand. It felt so natural. So comfortable. Why hadn't they done this sooner?

"There's something I want to tell you," he confessed.

Kennedy tried to look away from the melancholy sadness in his eyes. "You know you can tell me anything."

"I'm sorry I didn't mention everything sooner. I really

am. It was … it was stupid of me." He glanced down at the table.

She gave his hand a squeeze. "Don't worry about it."

"You shouldn't have had to find out the way you did. If I had just told you …"

"I'm sure it must have been hard. You know you didn't have to keep it a secret."

He shook his head. "I didn't want it to happen like this." A pause. Something in the way he looked at her pierced her spirit. "I really care about you."

She stared at their hands clasped together in the center of the table. "Me, too."

He glanced up at her. Pain shot out from his eyes, lanced her own soul. "I'm going back home when the semester's over."

She already knew that he was spending his summer break back in Kenya. Why was he telling her now? Why did he say it so seriously?

She glanced at his uneaten pizza, and then she knew.

"I won't be coming back next fall." His words were like a concrete ball sinking into an infinite depth.

Did she dare ask? "Why not?"

He stirred the ice in his Coke. "My dad lost his job when the government turned over. I can't afford to stay here."

"I thought you had a full scholarship."

"It doesn't cover flight expenses and things." He didn't look at her. "My family just can't pay for all that right now."

She swallowed past the lump in her throat, unable to picture a single day at Harvard without him. "What about your studies? What about becoming a doctor?"

"I can take classes in Nairobi. It's no big deal."

No big deal? Maybe that was easy for him to say. Maybe he could move away without feeling as if his internal viscera had gotten dropped into a paper shredder.

She certainly couldn't. "Why don't you talk to Carl and Sandy? I'm sure they'll let you spend the summers with them. They won't even charge you rent if you just explain ..."

"That's not all." There was a strain in his voice she'd never heard before. "I'm doing this because it's the best thing for us."

His words were like a punch in the gut.

He let go of her hand and stared at the table. "The longer I stay in Cambridge, the harder it's going to be when I ..." He choked and took a sip of Coke. "I'm sick. I may have another year, I may have twenty. But one day, this disease is going to kill me."

"Everyone dies sometime." It was a stupid thing to say. She realized that as soon as the words passed her lips.

"If I had my way," he began, "if I could choose exactly how this story ends, it would mean you and me graduating, going on to medical school." He cleared his throat. "Together. But I can't drag you through that with me. I can't risk getting you sick, putting you through ..." He stopped. "I have to go."

Did he mean at the end of the semester, or did he mean right now?

"People with HIV can still be in relationships." She didn't admit she had already done the research, already found websites devoted to helping couples where one partner was living with HIV. It wouldn't be easy, but it couldn't be as impossible as goodbye.

"I can't hurt you like that." He shook his head. "I won't." Tears streaked down his cheeks. She'd never seen him cry before. "Whatever happens, I need you to remember that I'm doing this for you."

Her throat seized up. "What if that's not what I want?"

"You have an amazing future ahead of you. A future helping others, healing others. You are the smartest person I know, the most talented. You're going to graduate from medical school and have your choice of any residency in the country. I'm not ..." He cleared his throat once more. "I'm not going to stop you from achieving that. I care about you too much. I ..." He let out his breath.

Kennedy leaned toward him, ready to catch his words.

"I just don't want to hurt you."

It didn't make sense. Five years from now, ten years from now, Kennedy knew it still wouldn't make sense. She should change his mind. Tell him how she really felt. Tell him all her dreams of medical school and residencies were pointless if he wasn't there by her side, goofing off with her in the lab, joking with her during their late nights in the library cramming for tests. She couldn't do any of that without him. Couldn't even make it through a stupid pizza dinner without crying.

She wiped her face. "You don't have to do this," she whispered.

He passed her a napkin. "I know. But I …" His voice caught again. "I want you to make me a promise."

She glanced up at his glistening eyes. "Yeah?"

"I want you to promise me that you'll remember this. Remember what we went through. Remember how many other people's lives are torn apart by diseases. You're a brilliant student. You're going to be a brilliant doctor. And I want you to promise me that you'll help them. Help the others so they don't have to go through something like this."

Her throat threatened to clench shut. "And what about you?"

"I'm going back home. I'll still keep up my studies. I don't know how, but I'll manage. I'll read every single journal article on AIDS research. And the day there's a cure, the day doctors tell me this disease isn't a death sentence, the day they tell me I can have a family of my own without having to worry about infecting the people I love, if you haven't moved on, you'll be the first person I call. Deal?"

She sniffed, still unable to believe this conversation was actually happening. She had a better feeling for how Aida felt in that underground vault as the air supply slowly, mercilessly disappeared.

"Deal."

He reached into his backpack. "I got you a present."

Kennedy's hands shook as she unwrapped the small package. "*The Last Battle?*"

"You remember what they always repeat at the end, don't you?" he asked.

Kennedy laughed through her tears.

"Further up and further in," they said at the same time.

"That's the kind of life I want you to have. The kind with new adventures, new discoveries every single semester. Every single day. It's what you deserve, and it's more than I can promise you. I …" He flipped the front cover open. "I wrote you a note."

Kennedy wondered how she was supposed to make out the words if her vision was so blurry. She wiped her eyes and read his inscription.

To my dearest friend Kennedy. Thank you for giving me the best year of my life. All my love, Reuben.

He had scooted his chair around so he was beside her now. Hugging her. Their tears intermingled on each other's faces.

"I wish you would stay here," she whispered.

He turned his face and kissed the very corner of her mouth. She couldn't tell if it was on her lips or on her cheek. She squeezed her eyes shut, begging God to pause time and let her and Reuben stay here forever.

"You know why I can't do that, don't you?" He kissed her once more.

Kennedy nodded. Some things didn't have to be said.

ACKNOWLEDGEMENTS

This is another novel that wouldn't have come into existence without the prayers, encouragement, and practical support of a whole team of friends. Annie, thanks again for the fabulous edits! If it weren't for you, Sandy would still be calling Kennedy "Sweatheart," and Willow would be struggling with the moose she put in her hair. Elizabeth, your proof-reading skills are exceptional, and I really have come to treasure our friendship. Thanks, Anne, for bringing the VW bus into existence and giving such helpful feedback, and Regi for always being such a great sounding board. A big shout-out also to my prayer team for putting up with so many (sometimes rambling) emails when I need your intercession. My husband remains my biggest fan and encourager, and none of my words would ever be written or have any meaning whatsoever if it weren't for the grace of my Lord Jesus.

I try not to shy away from controversial subjects in my writing, but I was worried when it came to drafting *Policed*. More than anything, I was afraid my readers would confuse my characters' political views for my own. My purpose in writing *Policed* was to raise questions, not to espouse a certain ideology. Several characters in this novel have strong opinions on issues of race relations, the police force, etc., and I hope that the issues you read about in *Policed* sparked some good discussions or internal musings. I also hope you found some encouragement and entertainment in the story itself. I had no other intention besides this.

I wrote the story of Spencer, the little boy whom the Lindgrens fostered, in memory of my friend's son Spencer who died before his family could hold him and tell him how much he was loved. I'm convinced he knew it anyway.

I dedicate this novel to the men and women who selflessly and courageously serve on police forces, keeping the peace and putting your lives on the line to protect the public. May God bless you in your work and keep you safe indeed.

DISCUSSION QUESTIONS

For group study or personal reflection

I always love to hear when a book club has decided to read one of my novels together! If you have a group of friends that would like to discuss *Policed*, I have included some discussion questions for you. They are organized based on how deep into the novel (and how potentially controversial) your group wants to go. This is entirely up to your personal group dynamics!

If you don't have a book club, these still might make for some fun introspective questions to journal or ponder. I always enjoy hearing from readers, and you're welcome to contact me any time at alanaterrybooks@gmail.com with feedback on any of my stories.

Ice Breaker Questions

1. Where is someplace where you always feel at home like Kennedy does at the Lindgrens'?

2. What was your favorite kids' book when you were growing up? What books would you include in the required reading list if you were Kennedy's children's lit professor?

3. If you could take any college or continuing ed class, what would you want to study?

4. What was your most memorable encounter with law enforcement that you're comfortable sharing?

Story-Related Questions

1. What did you think of Sandy's advice to marry your best friend?

2. Were you surprised by the ending? Do you think Reuben and Kennedy made the right decisions?

3. What would you have done if you were Kennedy and learned about Reuben's condition?

4. Have you ever had a memorable prayer encounter like Kennedy had with Dominic?

5. When have you witnessed or experienced prejudice or racism?

Political Questions *(Note: These questions are by their very nature controversial, and you may decide to skip them altogether based on your group's dynamics. My novels are only meant to foster discussion, never to sow discord. If you do go through these with a group, please be respectful of others' opinions, experiences, and beliefs with the understanding that there are no "right" answers.)*

1. Would you classify what happened to Kennedy and Reuben as a hate crime?

2. Pastor Carl, the youth pastor Nick, and Willow's friend Othello each have different opinions on the problem of race in America. Which position (if any) do you agree with most?

3. What is the most racially-charged historical or current event that you've lived through?

4. Do you believe that there's a race problem in your local community today?

5. In your opinion, what role do journalists and the media play in improving or straining race relations?

Books by Alana Terry

North Korea Christian Suspense Novels

The Beloved Daughter

Slave Again

Torn Asunder

Flower Swallow

Kennedy Stern Christian Suspense Series

Unplanned

Paralyzed

Policed

Straightened

Turbulence

See a full list at www.alanaterry.com